MOON

About this Book

Only *Flash What?* and *Gerry's Comeback* are connected. The rest of the 'Flashes' are a motley collection I've come up with in and out of lockdowns over the last 2 years and a couple as far back as February 2018 when I first heard of *Flash Fiction*.

Most are nothing more than a bit of fun or light drama. There are however, two seriously dark tales squeezed in there – the intros are there to give you a clue – I'd suggest you read them!

About the Author

Born in the Midlands (or 'God's own country' as Nat in *Not many Elephants* puts it) she and her siblings were dragged away in the 80's to the Isle of Man (Where's that?) where she's since discovered she liked it enough to stay.

Married with a blended family of 2 grown up sons, her interests include kayaking, walking, singing and cycling.

You can contact her via evieb@lifescape.im

MOONTIDE

The Flash Tales

The Library – Part 1: Flash *What*?	7
Carpe Diem	11
A Rose by any other Name	15
Isabella	19
Mastery	23
The Chosen One	27
Games of Chance	31
Iphigenia	35
Margo	39
Whose turn to Cook?	43
Belle	47
Doubting Thomas	51
Master and Commander	55
The Library – Part 2: Gerry's Comeback	59
Adjustments (to Landscape: Noon)	63

The Short Stories

Pigs in Blankets   67

Moontide   75

Not many Elephants…   95

Out soon

Opening chapters from *Wake me*…   145

MOONTIDE

*Intro – **The Library** – Part 1*

A little bit of mischief!

Between them, Gerry and Connell encapsulate some of my own experiences and struggles with the discipline needed for Flash. What a fuss! But Gerry's not easily defeated and gets the last laugh, as you'll see in Part II.

MOONTIDE

The Library – Part 1: Flash What?

Delia had suspected Gerry would never engage with the process.

Now Connell was standing behind Gerry, entertaining Delia with his best impression of him, books shoved under his jumper to add a paunch as he twiddled the ends of an imaginary handlebar moustache.

A published author of ten full length thrillers, some of them Bestsellers… Gerry continued

'Why would anyone want to read a story that short, let alone to write one! Blame it on Social Media myself… you can't fit a story into 250 words… ridiculous!'

'It's just a challenge, Gerry, a bit of fun really. Help yourself to some coffee… competition's open till tomorrow.'

She had his attention; the moustache was being stroked.

'Look, just write a short, simple story about anything you want. Don't count the words but bear in mind your next task will be weeding out anything extraneous. Go and sit with Connell, he's lost too!'

'Stuff and nonsense…' muttered Gerry to Connell an hour later, consigning a script that stubbornly refused to come in at less than 800 words to the bin, with

'I'm done… see you next week!'

Connell grinned, leaning on the counter as he whispered to Delia's Assistant, Lucy

'I'm sneaking off too… I've a Masters in English lit. from Durham and just downed five cups of coffee struggling to get less than 500 words myself.'

★ ★ ★

Ah well, horses for courses! Lucy anonymised her own effort before adding it to Delia's pile.

MOONTIDE

Intro – Carpe Diem

Seize the Day is one of my favourite expressions – though something I more often aspire to and don't always achieve. I haven't always got the guts (to carpe the diem, that is). Jess could be me at aged 14, not daring to speak to a boy I once fancied at school and knew from my friend's brother, liked me too.

Both painfully shy at the time, it needed one of us to take the plunge, but it didn't happen…

Mind you, he wasn't a patch on my Anglo-Indian hero, Nirvan.

If you want something, best go after it… unless it's illegal or going to cause major upset.

MOONTIDE

Carpe Diem

Jess was resolute: If she bottled it this time…

Last week she'd even thought about waving to him as the bus pulled away… then let her hand drop.

Last chance before the holidays anyway: Statement coat hastily pulled over her work things; a spritz of something to remember her by when, once again, she wafted past him without speaking.

As the bus approached, her eyes swept for any sign of him… There he was!

She resisted waving: Focus now Jess:

Bus half full – great!

Empty seat behind the target – excellent!

Now, just find some – any – pretext to talk to him!

Too late! While she hesitated, the pushy woman behind her squeezed past and beat her to it. The bus pulled out. Her heart sank as her target waved to a girl outside.

Jess flopped down in the seat in front of him, defeated, then, covering her watch with her sleeve, summoned her courage: About to turn and ask him the time, she was surprised to feel the gentlest tap on her shoulder.

Soft brown eyes held her embarrassed gaze.

'Hi… Nirvan… not a stalker… not usually! I was hoping the bus would be fuller so maybe you'd sit with me. We're the same stop, you and I… Time for a drink?'

MOONTIDE

MOONTIDE

Intro – A Rose by...

Don't you get fed up with people like Dan here?

He's shallow: In career terms he's clever and driven, but outside the office, no idea... just a superiority complex and a tendency to bray about where he's been and what he's done.

As someone who falls decisively into the Live to Eat camp, I dredged up some tasty ancient memories from my student year in France as the inspiration for a bit of gentle fun at the expense of Dan and his (equally toffee-nosed) mates.

Our heroine handles it gracefully though: After comments like that, I'd have been tempted to serve Dan's Beef Bugger-off (as my friend's Dad used to call it when I stayed for tea) straight into his lap.

Bon Appetit!

MOONTIDE

A Rose by any other Name

He'd overlooked that Chez Delphine would be closed. Dan's hopes of thanking Joe and Ben with dinner at his new favourite restaurant lay in tatters.

'Sorry Guys, it's the greasy spoon down the street then, nothing else this way.'

Pushing the door of the café and noticing the windows were open, he hoped the auburn-haired girl busy cleaning them hadn't caught his insensitive remarks.

For the last two hours, he'd been dreaming of Boeuf Bourguignon, all the time forgetting it was Tuesday.

'Table for three?'

She smiled, removing her gloves as she seated the guests.

'One moment … 'Dan detected a slight accent as, collecting three menus, she led them through to a courtyard furnished with easy chairs and lit by softly twinkling lights hidden amidst the climbing plants.

Shame the menu was less imaginative: Burgers or pizza.

Their hostess wandered back to take their order, frowning

'Sorry, I meant to mention the specials, assuming you're interested: Tonight's are Chicken Chasseur, Prawn Risotto or Braised Beef, each with a complimentary glass of wine… or a soft drink.'

Things were looking up as Dan and Ben opted for the beef, and Joe, the risotto. The wine was surprisingly drinkable, too: Beaujolais Villages – she'd left the bottle. As the kitchen door swung open and a familiar smell drifted out, another female voice broke through Dan's reverie.

'*Delphine*…tu viens m'aider, s'il te plaît'?

'Oui, Maman, j'arrives… deux minutes!'

MOONTIDE

MOONTIME

Intro – Isabella

Ballygally Castle is now a charming hotel along the Antrim Coast Road, not far from the Giant's Causeway. We stayed several years ago and heard tales of the ghost.

Isabella Shaw lived in the 1600's and her parents were keen for her to make an advantageous marriage: it didn't quite work out as they'd hoped.

Might want to pour yourself a drink before you read it: With the other stories, my aim was to entertain, make the reader smile or shove in a twist within the strict limit of 250 words, but this 'Flash' had a different aim. I'm a soppy soul but I've tried to convey a sense of how I felt when I visited Isabella's room (and again when I wrote this Flash).

Like Iphigenia (and cheese), this sad little Flash is best avoided last thing at night.

MOONTIDE

Isabella

'I heard her crying again last night, calling out for her baby' I told Reception.

'Okay to pick her some roses?'

★ ★ ★

A good match for an unremarkable girl like Isabella, he'd charmed her parents, but his eyes were hard, cruel even.

He used her dowry to finish 'their' house with its tower looking out over the sea. Isabella followed later, bringing the little dog.

For several long months they shared a room. The servants were kind, but Isabella was homesick.

With child, she was moved to a room high in the tower: A room… or a cell?

The maid, Mairi, begged Isabella not to cry, brought her roses from the garden, concealed her letter 'Father, HELP ME… '

But he intercepted the letter, replaced Mairi and removed the dog.

Mairi re-appeared for the confinement, brought fresh bedding, bathed Isabella's temples with rosewater.

She heard his cry! Perhaps now, her parents would visit? She fell asleep, contented.

★ ★ ★

They told her he'd died… yet Mairi walked on the beach daily, holding a small boy whose curls glinted red like Isabella's. He cried and her heart broke again.

★ ★ ★

He told them she'd thrown herself from the tower in her madness… or fell, attempting to escape.

We know better though, don't we Isabella?

Leaving the roses on the table and taking care to leave the door ajar, I tiptoe softly back down.

# MOONTIDE

MOONTIDE

Intro – Mastery

When the student is ready, the master will appear.

MOONTIDE

Mastery

Jesse was getting nowhere.

'Three months' Uncle Jed had said. 'Tame him; he's yours.'

With three weeks to go, it was the unspoken 'But if not…' troubling Jesse.

An icy resignation was settling as the pesky animal continued to monitor him from a distance, wheeling round the moment Jesse moved within a few yards.

If only he could make the colt understand the rancher had no use for passengers.

He shook the bucket but easing himself off the fence to drive the horse around the corral was predictably met once more with snorting and rolling eyes.

Removing a handful of nuts, Jesse sighed and hung the bucket in the corner, where the horse ignored it, waiting for him to disappear.

Reaching the fence and about to climb out though, Jesse suddenly found himself shunted forward.

'Quit messing, Sam…!' he began to say, but it wasn't his cousin as, to his astonishment, a chestnut muzzle appeared beneath his raised left arm, investigating the pocket of his jerkin.

His heart pounding, Jesse held his breath and slowly let his left arm fall as at the same time, he let his right hand run up the damply quivering neck, whispering softly and trying to breathe through his nose

'It's okay, you just wanted to show me who was boss; I get it!'

Meek as a lamb now, the red stallion followed Jesse back to the porch, where Uncle Jed looked on, scratching his head.

'Well, *I'll be* …!'

MOONTIDE

The Chosen One

This one grew out of my festive short story ('Pigs...), included later in this book.

The best laid plans, huh?

MOONTIDE

The Chosen One

A month now since Joe passed.

The pain confronted Julia each morning as she hit 'snooze' and turned to see the vacant space to her right. No thoughts of filling that Joe-shaped gap anytime soon but if she could only find something to focus on…

The sprawling colonial with its large yard and orchard had been their home for the past 20 years and as Kat returned to the kitchen, she was smiling: Julia had insisted on her exploratory visit *before* setting her heart on any dogs at the shelter.

'Any medium size dog really, small enough to lift into the Jeep when I go upstate, but preferably one who enjoys a good walk'.

Three days on and, Julia was chatting with Declan the vet, as, anxiously awaiting Kat's return, she took a seat on the bench beside the counter.

Suddenly the door opened and no sooner had Kat greeted Julia than a large, hairy (and decidedly damp) tornado launched himself at her, licking her cheek as huge muddy paws left their imprint on the cashmere sweater.

'Bruno! *Julia, I'm so sorry…*'

As Julia inspected the damage, Kat was doing her best to regain control of the St Bernard. Small chance now of their fussy British prospect taking any dog home. But just then, their well-dressed visitor stunned them both as she burst out laughing, wiping her eyes.

'Whatever I said, Guys, ignore it: Seems Joe sent me a message!'

MOONTIDE

Intro – Games of Chance

High Stakes card games come with a degree of risk and this one's no exception.

MOONTIDE

Games of Chance

Serra inspected her arm for bruises. Best the long sleeves this evening then, or there'd be another.

Her bold plan put both their lives at risk but looked their only way out – Serra knew too much.

'No limits tonight, Serenella' Fournier warned her 'Coin, gold, stock… Just deal and keep their glasses charged'.

Four around the table this evening, though it seemed both the Major and Doctor Norris were off their game tonight.

Three rounds in and the kitty already a thousand guineas: Time now to put those lessons from Fournier to good use. Serra bided her time.

Five rounds now, and as Sebastian hovered one card from triumph or disaster, her lace-trimmed sleeve accidentally caught the Doctor's glass, sweeping it from the table.

'Blundering Idiot! I'm so sorry Doctor…' grumbled Fournier

'Raise you… for the landau?' Sebastian interjected, patting his pockets and nodding towards the carriage and pair; his cousin's, it already hid the small bag holding everything of value to Serra.

'But of course, Viscount!' Fournier's mood changed in an instant. He'd seen enough of Sebastian's hand in the hidden mirror just two minutes earlier. But as Fournier lifted the curtain to admire the elegant barouche and Serra crouched to recover the broken glass, she tucked the Queen of Hearts into Sebastian's boot, before disappearing to the kitchens.

'All done, Gentlemen? I give you a straight flush!'

Fournier's triumph was short lived though, as Sebastian flipped his cards over to reveal a Royal Flush.

MOONTIDE

MOONTIDE

Intro – Iphigenia

Men and women throughout history have done some appalling, evil and unnatural things in the name of religion, but for Agamemnon, 'misguided' doesn't quite cut it. He was a King of kings, the unchallenged leader of 'Team Greece', proud, egotistical and answerable to nobody.

I can still remember my 'A' level Latin class years on – Mr Rawlinson could quite easily have changed his suit and tie for a toga as he read out loud those chilling words written by Lucretius more than 2,000 years ago, the lengths a powerful ruler would go to, to placate the Gods and encourage them to send the wind he needed to launch his 1,000 ships.

And Lucretius wasn't just a poet, he understood clever scientific stuff we now know as Atomism, Kinetic Particle Theory and Brownian Motion!

MOONTIDE

Iphigenia

Ten years he had waited to avenge Menelaus!

Blood was blood, a brother's shame stung as Agamemnon's own and Priam's Troy, with its seven shining towers, majestic, glorious and impregnable, was soon to be obliterated, erased from history, every last citizen slaughtered.

First though, there remained one unpleasant duty.

★ ★ ★

'*Me*... to be the wife of Achilles, Father? I am truly blessed!'

Barefoot, Iphigenia entered the temple in her robe of white silk, her golden hair plaited with flowers, eyes wide as she marvelled at its splendour... then, momentarily perplexed, enquiring

'Where is Achilles, Father?'

A last wave of doubt, of paternal affection, of regret, but he'd long delayed and the Gods must be appeased.

'Have patience my child; He comes presently. Now, approach the altar.'

Excited and trembling, she hesitated – a premonition? – soon dismissed as Father forced a smile, holding out his hand so that Iphigenia relaxed, trusted, knelt just as Father asked, closed her beautiful eyes in prayer for the last time.

She belonged to him, this daughter, his first born and what use was a daughter, if not to forge alliances with bordering lands; with one's enemies; *with the Gods?*

Swiftly and silently the blades fell, washing Artemis' sacred shrine with the guiltless blood.

Tantum Religio potuit suadere malorum ★

★Such are the crimes – too dreadful to speak of – to which Superstition can drive humankind.

Titus Lucretius Carus – 'On the Nature of Things'

MOONTIDE

MOONTIDE

Intro – Margo

Four of my Flashes are named after women. The other characters bring with them some type of drama but this gentle flash is just an unassuming slice of life with a small twist.

MOONTIDE

MOONTIDE

Margo

Margo yawned as she sat looking out of the window.

Roberta was compulsive, picking the same things up, vacuuming underneath, before putting them down again.

As she waited, the only excitement to be found was in two raindrops racing down a window, though, just as they were inches from the bottom, predictably, Roberta began fussing again.

'Shift while I do that bit again...' And before you knew it, Margo found herself gently shoved aside while Roberta felt the carpet beneath the window... before passing the vacuum over it again.

Suddenly though, things were looking up.

'Rain's stopped... fancy a walk?'

Margo didn't need asking twice. She waited by the front door, another ten while Roberta tried on – and rejected – three different jackets, before settling on the first.

Car keys located, as Roberta checked her lipstick for the Nth time, Margo caught the fleeting smile of apology. She hoped Barry and Jim might be around now it was getting late. Roberta was fonder of Barry than she'd yet dared admit to her sister, though Margo secretly approved. She loved nothing more than relaxing outside at 'The Bell' while they all caught up, before returning to their self-imposed confinement three floors up.

A pair of mallards by the lake quacked indignantly and took flight as the walkers passed.

Later, as Barry and Roberta sat enjoying their cider and crisps, their two Labradors snoozed companionably beneath the table.

MOONTIDE

MOONTIDE

Intro – Whose turn to Cook?

So I'm obsessed with food… good food, proper food, none of your nouvelle cuisine for me. If I want something pretty to look at I'll buy a painting, thanks: You can stick your foams and your jus' where the sun don't shine!

There are some great places to eat in and around Belfast; ranging from humble cafés where you leave a donation to something a bit more upmarket and one of my favourites serving Bistro type scram is just walking distance from the Titanic Quarter. We've sat there time and again over drinks, tongues hanging out as we counted and recounted how much we had to last the rest of our stay. A couple of times, though, we did stay to eat – superlative on every level!

MOONTIDE

Whose turn to Cook?

We'd enjoyed our chat with the man on the next table. Not someone who easily blended into the background with the long white hair and beard. The renowned local artist – whose name momentarily escaped us – chatted with us until the waitress bustled over to announce his table was ready.

Stretching out our beers, we watched him disappear upstairs to the dining room as we enviously pondered which ready meal would do us for tea.

Those seven days before payday are the cruellest, no contest. We did our best to ignore the delicious aromas wafting by with each plate exiting the kitchen.

But then, the chef appeared down the spiral stairs he'd climbed not two minutes before. Carrying a plate which was clearly untouched, he was cursing and shaking his head

'Won't you just look at this: Celebrities huh? Ted's in every week and half the time, he changes his mind.

'Fillet steak with peppercorn sauce, please Declan'… so it was. That was half an hour ago though, and now he wants fish!

Looks like steak for supper again… unless… are you hungry? Such a waste, just to eat it myself.'

He had our attention as, encouraged by our eager faces, he disappeared in search of two forks.

Just enough to share, I'd say.'

MOONTIDE

MOONTIDE

Intro – Belle

All these short stories with their different characters... it's not that I've run out of names, just deliberately avoided using any here, to boost the 'transactional' feeling.

The idea behind this Flash came from the 1967 film 'Belle du Jour' directed by Luis Buñuel and starring Catherine Deneuve, later inspiring the ITV series 'Secret Diary of... which ran from 2007-11 and featured Billie Piper.

Luckily for her, our twenty-first century Belle is keen to stay mistress of her own destiny.

MOONTIDE

MOONTIDE

Belle

'Promise me you'll consider it?' he'd entreated as he left

'Spare key on the side there.'

The third time she'd seen him, planned with military precision; cocktails at 7:00pm with ample time to unwind before the short walk to Rules for 8:00. Then back to the apartment by 10.00 to watch a movie and alarm set for 6:00 am.

She could get used to the lifestyle, plenty of space for her car, rent for the garage alone would be more than the payments on her one-bed studio.

She couldn't fault him: Good looking in a deceptively boy-next-door sort of way; financially secure; apartment just off Bloomsbury Square; Jacobean mansion in the Cotswolds, all yellow sandstone and mullioned windows.

Trouble was, she wouldn't get to visit. As his permanent home, the Cotswolds served as home to his wife and three children in term time. Outside school terms and Parliamentary sittings, he decamped with them to Aspen or Marbella, depending on the season.

She'd be left alone, placated with meaningless gifts and the occasional call.

Consigning the draft NDA to the bin where she knew it belonged, she dialled the agency, before summoning the lift.

'It's B.... No, there's no problem... I honestly can't fault him, just find someone else next time he calls... tell him I left.'

MOONTIME

Intro – Doubting Thomas

It's a tough call for Thomas.

First the Church is selling the splendid Georgian pile Thomas has been privileged to call home for the past 20 years from under him and now his beloved daughter is about to arrive, bursting with a secret which will test the limits of her Dad's rejection of all things commercial and non-spiritual at Christmas!

Doubting Thomas

Two weeks to Christmas.

Thomas sighed as he lifted the curtain, glancing out across the snow. It wasn't the snow that bothered him, more that unmissable FOR-SALE sign hanging on the gate since yesterday. All the snow did was rub it in as the scene which greeted him this morning showcased the winter wonder of the Vicarage gardens.

He'd known the time would come and it didn't feel like 20 years; Angie seven when they arrived and Rufus, minus two months!

A move of 300 miles, that house had clinched the offer – Prelate of St Cuthbert's, or 'primate' as Rufus had once told his reception class teacher.

By Easter, home would be a soulless concrete box in town.

Thomas rebuked himself: Any Church being supposedly its congregation, not the building, the same must go for the Vicarage, surely?

Christmas Adverts blared out – all commerciality, no spirituality! Ever likely numbers were dwindling. Kids who didn't have it expecting X-Box or Play-Station; those who did, the latest games before they sold out.

The phone started ringing insistently. Dreading a viewing request, it was a relief to hear Angie

'Dad! You won't mind if we come two days early? Some news, too hot for the phone'.

A baby, maybe? His money was on that, Thomas's frown now chased away by a wide smile, though not as wide as Angie's spreading grin, holding tight to the winning ticket as she cut their videocall to dial the agent.

MOONTIDE

MOONTIDE

Intro – Master and Commander

Many of us will have learned a new skill during lockdowns, whether it's the basics of a foreign language, a new musical instrument, a few new recipes, or a (more-complicated than-it-looked) dance from Laurel and Hardy's **Way out West**.

When you've known someone – or known of them – since Primary School, don't be tempted to assume they no longer have the ability to surprise – or for that matter, to impress.

MOONTIDE

MOONTIDE

Master and Commander

Another month in lockdown, spiced up with an overnight curfew.

The first already a baptism of fire for couples like Flo and Ben, trying to keep energetic toddlers amused indoors 24-7 or tutoring teenagers in subjects they knew nothing about.

'Don't envy you, Mate!' Simon had empathised. The evenings though, must be tough for social types and count that double for Simon; no garden and suddenly confined five floors up! Ordinarily, Ben couldn't imagine him home before 10.00 pm more than two evenings a week, the rest divided between playing music or out networking and arranging concerts.

Simon still firmly on the competitive side of 'social'; smart and at times impatient, tending to brusque.

Ben was closing their computer, struggling to imagine Simon confined five floors up, when he stopped…

'FLO …come and look… you couldn't script it!'

A virtual Railway company, complete with realistic scenery and passengers? The stock, anything from tilting trains to the *Flying Scotsman*: and there in the centre of it all, Simon, welcoming his subscribers as they joined him from around a locked-down globe.

Simon, but not the Simon Ben knew. Relaxed and accommodating as his followers quickly passed 10,000, Ben and Flo sank transfixed into the sofa as diverse people mingled: Tonight, Students jostling virtual elbows with Fishermen, Chefs, a Submarine Commander and several Pilots, each vying for the prize of *Network Controller* for an evening.

'Look at this – What's next d'you reckon… kids, vineyard maybe?' said Ben.

MOONTIDE

MOONTIME

Intro – The Library II – 'Gerry's Comeback.'

*Gerry didn't take to the Librarian's little **Flash** challenge did he? Looking down on it from his lofty heights, you'd think it was sent for no other reason than to annoy him!*

BUT… He doesn't like anything to defeat him.

*Sandwiched somewhere in the middle of my forthcoming novel **Wake me at Wine Time** is a Legend I made up when I couldn't find one to fit: Gerry's nicked my story and condensed it into just a few lines.*

MOONTIDE

MOONTIDE

Gerry appeared with 5 minutes to go.

'You wanted Micro-fiction, Delia – Fill your boots!'

★ ★ ★

It was the fifteenth century with Erzebet now sole custodian of *Kiss Villány,* Edward having been taken last Winter by the Pestilence.

Why should she mourn him though when he'd gambled away her dowry with nothing left for the leaking roof? The only hope for her, Jakob and Maria was their productive wine land, those vines bordering the estates of their rival, Sir Istvan Vardas. He'd taken all the local labour, would see her ruined…

Paddling in the river, Erzebet could, if only for a moment forget her troubles as the lightest breeze ruffled her hair, and the sinking sun caressed her shoulders …

Just then, a voice disturbed her contemplation; a voice with a kindly countenance and deep grey eyes.

'A fine evening, my Lady… some wine perhaps?' He opened a flask engraved with the Lion of St Mark.

'*Matthias Vardas*… my father forbids my return to Venice, wishing to unsettle his neighbour, Sir Edward Foldessi'.

Erzebet frowned, summoning all the dignity she could muster whilst knee deep in water.

'To unsettle Edward, Sir, is to unsettle me for I am his widow and now sole support for two elderly servants.'

'Then… forgiving my boldness, but if Sir Edward is no more… and you might learn to share my fondness for Venice… we may have found a solution to both our problems.'

★ ★ ★

Delia beamed 'Crafty you, played me all along'

Adjustments (to Landscape: Noon)

Sophia continued to glare at the huge canvas, clearly troubled.

'Nearly finished, Uncle John? Only, it's not quite right'.

Precocious? In the nicest sense: Like John though, she had an instinct for landscapes.

'What's wrong, Sophia?' he smiled indulgently.

'Still too gloomy for midday… the greens are real enough, but it's crying out for a few touches in red, just to bring it to life'.

And she wasn't finished, pondering

'… and it needs some interest in the foreground' deliberating

'A dog maybe… how about a spaniel like *Snap*, just left of the area where you painted out that horse and rider?'

'Indeed!' The President and John's fellow exhibitors would have apoplexy at the Artist's being influenced by a 12-year-old girl, but John said nothing, simply dipped his brush and did precisely as Sophia had suggested.

Sadly, the *Royal Academy* were less impressed, critical over the messiness, the *scraping* on the reflected water and the artist's 'departure from established form'.

Sophia was desolate: In her quest for perfection, what trouble she had caused him! Her instinct, though, was to be proved right within 3 years when Uncle John triumphed at the Paris Exhibition of 1824, beating the French at their own game.

★ ★ ★

'*Incroyable*…a masterpiece!'

Delacroix stood in rapt contemplation of Constable's most talked-about canvas, destined to snatch the Gold Medal that year.

'Your illustrious '*Academy*' underestimated this painting, Monsieur. You my friend, have shown us all how landscapes should now be painted… with Courage and Truth.'

MOONTIDE

MOONTIDE

Adjustments – Postscript

It's no secret that John Constable made several revisions to his most famous painting now loved the world over as The Haywain. The most famous landscape in British Art certainly didn't impress the Royal Academy on its first outing, though ultimately caused a sensation in Paris (1824) where it carried off the Charles X Gold Medal, the most prestigious Art prize in Europe.

It's also understood that Delacroix (widely regarded as the leading French Artist of the Romantic movement) was very taken with Constable's work, which went on to influence him; in particular, in the way he painted his skies.

Sophia though – JC's meddlesome niece – is a pure figment of my imagination as is Snap, the dog!

MOONTIDE

Pigs in Blankets

Just as things were looking up and they'd reached the top of the list for first dibs on the garden flat, Geoff had shown Jo the letter, before, one week later, dropping the bombshell. She knew the company had offered him a promotion, but it depended on his moving back to the UK and after all that trouble to make a new life together in the States: No way was Jo retracing her steps across the Atlantic anytime soon!

With Christmas just over a week away and (since Jo declined to go with him), his plan was to fly back in time to spend the Festive Season with his family. Geoff's Dad had rented a cottage in Wales for three weeks over the Christmas period and from the moment she'd seen the photos, those views of Snowdonia and no neighbours for half a mile, she'd been looking forward to spending a few days there just after New Year.

If she was honest though, Jo was more disappointed and annoyed at Geoff's shock announcement than sad at splitting with Geoff. Things had been cooling for some time; she'd sensed it without either the energy to question or the inclination to stoke the fire. They'd taken that first, brave step together, 18 months ago. As their friends settled in and around London, Manchester or Liverpool snapping up opportunities with Solicitors ranked highest in the Legal 500, the intrepid pair had instead taken a leap in the dark. Flights to JFK and no firm job offers had left them with pooled savings just shy of £2,000.

Now Jo felt alone and let down. Mum and Dad would be flying out to stay with them – her, she corrected herself – on 20 January , though she had been looking forward to a long weekend with them in Chester, before joining Geoff's folks in Wales for another four days.

Geoff could go with her blessing and though they'd likely stay in touch for a while, it was clear they had less and less in common.

Thinking about it, he'd always been the more driven and that had ramped up in the last year as, once he'd found his feet, he'd taken full advantage of 'the City that never sleeps' to work the 60-hour weeks on offer and rack up any associated bonuses. Jo, in contrast, already preferred to work smart rather than hard, primarily from home these days. That meant she could walk in Central Park almost daily. For her, quality of life already counted way more than dollars in the bank… assuming she could meet the bills after Geoff left.

He'd been totally straight with her in fairness: Shown her the letter a month ago, and she knew the interview (by remote link) had gone okay. He'd known of the offer for a fortnight and there seemed an unspoken assumption Jo would go with him: She could always find a job when she got there – whether a serious job or a 'hobby job' as he put it. Jo couldn't picture herself like the wives of some of Geoff's friends, several of them already busy with kids. Whilst she loved kids, she was in no rush for her own yet, though it was clear from hints Geoff's folks had been dropping they were anxiously awaiting the next chapter, the one with the statutory 2.6 kids, golf club membership, fashionably muddy RUV and all the circus that went with the sort of life they – and now Geoff – envisioned.

'FLIP IT…' Jo reproached herself '… the guy's actually done you a favour!'

It was just the timing that stank.

The outlook for Christmas might be bleak, then, but Jo was determined to stay in New York. She smiled at the thought that if she could do Christmas alone in this of all places and carve out some fun, she'd feel quite smug. She'd probably do some sort of volunteering over the holidays; she'd start looking into it that very evening. And assuming she could still afford the garden flat

PIGS IN BLANKETS

(she'd take a lodger if she needed to, only slightly put off by Single White Female). Something else on the list, though was a dog: No make or model, just a small, friendly dog who'd be happy sharing the new garden flat in Greenwich Village.

Jo wasn't new to volunteering either. Not long after she and Geoff had arrived, she'd helped for a couple of weeks in an animal shelter just three blocks away. Giving something back while waiting to land a proper job, she'd only stopped when she landed an in-house position with a Publisher in Manhattan, their tiny office with its sought-after 'Uptown' location.

With Jo's job, she got to spend most days at home, was happy just where she was and would be made up when she could move into the garden flat straight after New Year.

No question about it: Jo was staying put – if she'd ever had doubts, the option on the garden flat had made it a no-brainer.

With 'Project-Doggie-Adoption' firmly in view, she picked up the phone, checked her contacts for the shelter she'd helped at and pressed go…

'Yes?'

The voice sounded impatient, busy, someone with better things to do than speak to her. She thought she detected an accent, but too early to say.

'Hi, it's Joanna Rivers. I'd like to come by and discuss homing one of your rescue dogs. A puppy or a dog is fine, not a Newfoundland or a German Shepherd though, it would need to be quite a bit smaller, Mr ……?'

'Doktor Baranovsky, Sacha. You can come by at 3:30, Mrs. Rivers?'

Russian?… both the accent and the name suggested Russian.

'Miss Rivers, actually – Yes, I'll be happy to, but…'

'Thank you… See you then.'

And with that, the phone went down.

★ ★ ★

Not a moment before 3.29pm, Jo rang the bell (as the sign still instructed) and walked into reception. As the student manning the desk smiled and rose to greet her, the door to the operating theatre flew open and a nurse emerged, followed by a veterinarian pushing a small dog on a trolley, eyes flickering indicating him to be in recovery, his topmost hind leg almost entirely covered by a bandage.

Tall with auburn hair and beard, the imperious man in green scrubs, now removing his mask had to be Doctor Baranovsky as, ignoring their visitor, he called out to the receptionist.

'Amelia, would you assist Katherine with Max' adding, more gently 'Just make sure he has water and keep an eye on him. I'll check him in half an hour.'

'Can I help?' Jo offered. 'I did several weeks here last year with Doctor Brodie – Declan – He was in charge then.'

The vet managed a smile as he threw his discarded mask into the bin behind the counter, closely followed by his cap.

'Thank you, but not necessary… Miss….?'

'Rivers…Joanna Rivers… You said to come at three-thirty.'

'Ah, I remember. You would like to offer a home to one of our dogs. One moment, please, while I find the diary.'

Jo was familiar with the drill. Homes were checked out before the person offering to adopt chose a dog, or occasionally, the dog chose them. She laughed remembering a woman, Julia, then recently widowed, who'd been set on a small to mid-size dog… before being bowled over with love by a St Bernard. She'd since met Julia and Bruno a few times walking in the Park and the smile said it all, but it could have gone a different way: Bruno had introduced himself by climbing onto the bench beside Julia and licking her face while at the same time, wiping his mud-spattered paws on her expensive sweater! Lucky that Julia had the space, time – and the funds – to care for him.

Jo sank down again, as it hit her: just one week to go before Christmas!

'So, Miss Rivers… when can we visit? I can offer you 2 January if that suits…'

'Jo, please Dr. Baranovsky… and would it be possible to squeeze me in before Christmas? I know it's a big ask…'

'Let's see… and Sacha, please'. He continued to leaf through, frowning… 'As you can see, my diary is already full with visits for the animals. Those with medical issues… Katherine's happy to handle the others before she takes off… Plus there are… procedures.' Jo must have looked troubled for a second, before remembering that the shelter never euthanised a healthy animal. Dr Baranovsky had obviously noticed though, miming the action of 'snipping' to reassure her.

'Ah, I see!'

'These routine operations, appointments and emergencies will take me right up to Christmas Eve. Then again from 27 December… I'm sorry.' Sacha shrugged before continuing.

'Left to me, I'd offer you Christmas Day but I'm on duty here, looking after our residents while my colleagues stay home with their families… or disappear to the Hamptons… he glanced towards Katherine – Ouch!

Poor man! Jo's empathy was in full flow

'Don't you at least get chance to spend time with your family later in the day… Roast turkey, mulled wine, pulling crackers… silly games and stuff?'

'NIET… no turkey, no crackers, no wife… no family in USA. After I leave here, microwave dinner, TV then sleep…'

Even as she'd blurted it out, she had to admit this man didn't look the silly-games type. Jo was struggling to imagine him playing Twister, or that daft game of Guess my Name, not for a moment. How trivial it would all seem to him... Best shut up.

But then, reminded of her own enforced solitude looming over Christmas, a random spontaneous notion came to her and before she could stop herself, Jo had offered...

'Dr Baranovsky – Sacha – by coincidence, my own plans for Christmas Day have just fallen through. I was expecting to cook for other people, which means I've got loads of food. How about I come and help you for a couple of hours, check on the little guy you just operated on, him with the bad leg.

Once the dogs are happy, I'll be able to show you a traditional British Christmas dinner; Turkey, stuffing, bread sauce, pigs in blankets... I'm less than 20 minutes away so I'll bring it all with me – I can cook everything the day before'.

'Sounds good... but what are these...pigs?' he enquired; eyebrows drawn together, clearly befuddled as he imagined a load of eccentric English folks absorbed in some fun game that involved rolling pigs around in blankets.

In fairness to Sacha, Amelia was looking equally perplexed, though Katherine was giggling, doing her best to explain as Jo continued to sell the idea to him.

'Glad you rescued me there, Katherine! While Sacha is mulling over my offer though, I wasn't thinking: It really depends on your still having that old microwave in the kitchen, only I'll need something to cook the Christmas pud as well as for warming the food.'

The way Sacha had lit up, you'd have thought she'd just offered to pay off his mortgage, not share a meal and throw in a couple of hours help with the dogs... as he beckoned.

'Come with me – the old microwave gave up; I found a better

one, see?'

Jo followed him through to the back and once she'd inspected the new microwave, he shook her hand, holding onto it as he went on

'*Miss* Rivers (his emphasis here on the Miss, just as she'd said it on the phone) Joanna... I'd be lying to say I'm sorry your plans fell through. Your Christmas is spoiled whereas mine just got better: Now, I'll be looking forward to your company, your Christmas pudding – and your pigs in their blankets – on Christmas Day!'

'Sorted then! I'll try and be here before Noon. I'll call if there's any delay, the Shelter's number's already in here...' tapping her phone.

'One moment... your number, please?'

As Sacha texted her his private cell number, she thought that was it for today, but reaching for the door, there was one last thing.

'I'll be off-duty all day Boxing Day. Declan's covering, so, if you're free, I could squeeze in your home visit then? Max there – his despondent face reminds me of my Uncle, Maxim – will be looking for a new home as soon as that leg starts to mend.

... I have an idea your place might be just what he's after.'

THE END

MOONTIDE

Moontide

Jack was 10 now, almost 11. He picked up on more than Sadie realised.

It was a year since Kayden (and Jack) had moved in together and Jack had noticed that Mum and Kayden were rowing more of late. Most often it was Sadie who started the rows, she could pretty much argue with herself.

Jack had met Kayden a few times before he moved in with them. Ordinarily, Jack was disoriented by changes but had no issue when Mum asked, after 6 months of seeing Kayden, whether he minded Kayden moving in. Jack had liked Kayden from the start, Heck, even his Dad, Phil, liked Kayden, who had 3 grown-up children of his own. Kayden had somehow managed to tread the fine line between being caring and supportive to his partner's only child whilst at the same time not once pushing Jack's Dad's nose out or creating the impression he was trying to 'steal' his son.

Fair to say that Jack was sad at any thought of Sadie and Kayden splitting up though aside from Kayden's company, what he'd miss most whenever Kayden tired of his Mum's tantrums, was the boat. Kayden's yacht the *Jon Trelawny* was magnificent, less a yacht, more a ship in miniature. Together, Kayden and his beloved boat had circumnavigated half the globe. Jack wondered if that experience – plus the fact he had for a time taught kids of Jack's age – might explain Kayden's laid-back attitude to life and his skill in diffusing Sadie's regular attempts to needle him.

Even at his age, Jack got that not much was going to phase you in life once you'd sailed the Atlantic single-handed, faced fifty-foot waves in the Southern Ocean, typhoons at sea, system failures, torn sails, a shortage of drinkable water and a nail-biting temporary repair mid-Atlantic after suffering a broken mast!

What Jack really appreciated on top of Kayden's heroics though, was Kayden's understanding of kids like him. Kids with special needs, in Jack's case a degree of Autism 'just a spoonful,' Kayden would say, waving it away as if it were of no consequence.

Kayden wasn't going to let a little thing like Autism get in the way of Jack's having adventures in a boat. He'd seen plenty of children with a higher spectrum version of something similar to Jack and shared the determination of both Sadie and Philip – Jack's Dad – that the youngster should never become nervous to venture outside. He'd known a few who'd foregone outdoor activities in favour of hours spent at a computer: Something that would never happen to Jack on his watch!

Kayden had told Jack soon after they met how his eldest son, Michael, challenged for a while by similar issues at Jack's age, was now 26 and had a very exciting job. He hoped Mikey might be flying out to visit them soon. Currently though, he was busy with some ground-breaking scientific work for a company based in Boston, Massachusetts, just South of where Kayden hailed from.

Jack was mad keen to meet Mikey and hear more about his work, even more so when Kayden mentioned how the job involved very little time sitting in the office and lots of travel and underwater exploration. He'd never dreamed jobs like that existed! Most of his friends' parents worked in shops or offices, though a few now worked from home, a reluctant flexibility introduced since the Covid Lockdowns, which at least helped them squeeze out more of a family life.

Mikey's job, though, was something else and sounded far more like one long holiday. Jack assumed Mikey must have been 'cured' of his anxiety but when he mentioned it to Kayden, he laughed and shook his head.

'Not cured, Dude: No magic cure, he just learned to *manage* it.'

That made Mikey a superhero in Jack's book, even more so when Kayden added

'You can do it too, but it takes practice. It'll be hard at first, and although I can help you, the rest has to come from you.'

★ ★ ★

Kayden knew that the boat would be a great advantage in building Jack's confidence, just as it once had for Mikey.

On the 'Jon T' (as Kayden affectionately called the 50-foot blue-water cruiser, explaining why anyone from the US would howl at Jack's suggestion

'Why not shorten it to *the Jon?*')

safety was paramount; more so when considering a young person with special needs.

Kayden eased Jack in gently, letting him help with little jobs on board, saying it would take his mind off any thoughts of seasickness. Jack felt secure around Kayden, whether on land or at sea; always making sure that Jack had his lifejacket on before starting the engine and moving the boat off its berth, even in a Marina. He was patient showing Jack and his Mum the locations of the safety lines positioned at intervals on the deck, checking their harnesses and demonstrating how to clip on before he'd allow either one outside the cockpit whilst at sea.

Kayden had also given Jack a watch, which (so he claimed) was waterproof to 200 metres. (Curiously, the dial just said 50 metres, but Jack preferred to believe Kayden).

When the boat was behaving and conditions were good, Kayden would turn off the engine so that Jack could for a time experience the magic that can only ever be felt in a sailing ship. At the same time though, Kayden had warned him (and Jack had already experienced) just how on a beautifully sunny day with next to no wind, a gust could suddenly appear out of nowhere to snatch at the mainsail like a huge wild beast, causing 20 tons of boat to pitch and roll.

Kayden promised Jack that once Mikey was with them, they'd go sailing and Mikey would demonstrate a special trick: the mystical manoeuvre known as 'heave-to' which made the boat stop dead as if clutched by a giant hand and set down in an invisible, sheltered parking spot right in the middle of the Ocean! Meanwhile and whenever Kayden had the slightest suspicion of the wind's creeping up or the sea state's being other than smooth (whether from the shipping forecasts or the onboard GPS plotter) he'd have a 'reef' in the sails as a precaution before you could say 'pass the wrench'!

Kayden's time as a lone sailor had taught him to be ready at half a minute's notice to turn the boat down-wind and lash the wheel to a particular compass point, riding things out till the worst of the storm had passed.

Sadie was a learner, too, she'd been out in the *Jon T* a couple more times than Jack but as Kayden confided,

'You're doing great – Mum's not as brave, nor as quick a learner.'

Always a *day-sailor* before mutual friends had (nervously) introduced her to Kayden, it had been quite a coup when Kayden and Jack had craftily persuaded Sadie to 'a gentle cruise' round the Cornish coast for a long weekend: Valuable practice for their current adventure!

On this trip though, Kayden's plan was to head over to France, assuring Jack it was 'just a hop' after the journeys he and the *Jon T* had achieved together.

This time, it would be good if they ended up somewhere just South of the Brest Peninsula. For now though, he'd aim for Cherbourg, after which they'd spend a few days gently creeping down the coast, as far as La Rochelle if conditions were good.

MOONTIDE

He'd shown Jack on the chart, adding that whilst they planned to complete the voyage in around a week before starting their passage home, it might be quicker if conditions were as good as he anticipated.

Kayden had been impressed with how Jack had taken to the boat, especially with no prior experience beyond the small motor launch Phil had bought to ferry him and his visitors to and from the Island in the Lake District he currently rented from the National Trust.

★ ★ ★

So tonight, they were lying at anchor at a popular hopping-off point just off the South Coast, out in the bay not far from Poole. Conditions were great but promised to be even better once they made landfall, whether in Normandy or Brittany.

Kayden had already satisfied himself everything was as it should be but returned on deck once more to assure himself the *Jon T's* anchor was secure in its overnight bed of sand and rocks before he and Sadie retired to the port-side cabin for a few hours. By now, Jack had already been asleep in his cosy little bunk on the starboard side for more than two hours.

Hearing the saloon clock beep its reminder at 11:00 pm, Kayden hastened back down and rinsed their coffee mugs.

Gently nudging a sleepy Sadie, curled up on one of the benches in the saloon, he'd tempted her with the promise that if she came to bed right now, he'd do a solo safety check during the night. He knew she'd be less grouchy on five hours undisturbed sleep before it was time to eat a swift breakfast and lift the anchor.

So far, the August weather had been kind and everything was going okay aside from Sadie's occasional moodiness. When she was happy, Sadie was great company and a very good Mum, never forgetting to top-up the milk in Jack's beaker in the fridge. The old cup from his baby days (leading to Jack being teased when the school bully had upended his bag on the 'bus) had recently taken on a new status. Suitably 're-purposed', it was now a drinking vessel fit for the 'first mate' on the yacht that (to Jack) resembled a pirate ship.

All was quiet as somewhere on land, a church clock struck Midnight and soon after, a disoriented, thirsty boy wearing *Sponge-Bob* pyjamas emerged from his cabin into the saloon.

No need to disturb Mum and Kayden. Jack had already gulped half the deliciously cool milk when, mug tilted to take another sip, he paused and frowned, noticing the brass hook at the top of the stairs giving access to the outside.

Something wasn't right: Ordinarily, that small hook secured the hatch when pulled shut. Right now though, it hung loose, swinging with the gentle motion of the boat. (Kayden could only have forgotten to secure it when he'd returned on deck to double-check for plenty of resistance on the anchor before going back to sleep).

Imagine his embarrassment after reinforcing with Jack and Sadie – time and again – the importance of staying safe at sea! Not to worry though, on such a gorgeous, still, clear evening Jack, wide awake now, was bursting to get a better look at the moon. He'd pull the door shut and make sure the hook was back in place in a few minutes on his way back down. Meanwhile and wandering up the short stairwell, with both the door catch and the bolts each side unsecured, it was irresistible just to ease back the hatch and clamber over the door for another look at the beautiful, bright full moon.

An oversized and well-rounded moon, Jack'd been admiring it earlier through his prized binoculars, fast becoming a fixture around his neck most of the day. They'd been a last-minute present from Dad, in anticipation of the trip to France. Phil was as keen as anyone that the trip went well. He admired how Kayden showed such care both for his neurotic ex-wife and his autistic son: The tetchy Sadie, with her various neuroses and grumbling and Jack's condition calling for extra patience and reassurance. Kayden had levelled with Phil that, assuming nothing untoward on their trip, he was thinking of proposing to Sadie, keen to gauge his reaction first: Phil was delighted – Kayden's moving in with her and Jack had already lifted a great deal of the day to day worry away from him.

In the daylight, Jack never tired of watching the dolphins playing around the *Jon T*. He smiled at the pod having fun as they made the most of the water churned up and warmed by the boat's passage, their own fairground ride. Kayden had stood with Jack on the bow sprit, showing him how the pod of about 7 grey dolphins who'd stayed alongside for half an hour that afternoon would queue to swim off the port bow (front left) of the boat before swimming around to the stern, where they'd queue again, awaiting their next turn!

The boat was still now but might there still be any sign of them? – He'd seen a creamy-white flash and heard a splash in the distance just before settling down in his bunk and, as chance would have it, fallen asleep still wearing the binoculars!

Locating his *Crocs* under the navigation table just outside his cabin and slipping them on in case he trod on anything sharp, Jack tiptoed soundlessly up on deck, scissoring his legs over the low door. Crossing the cockpit and continuing along the gangway on the starboard side, he carefully removed the shoes before he stepped onto the wooden planks lining the foremost part of the boat, the bowsprit.

There it was again!

An arch of creamy gold with occasional flashes of silver and a distant SPLASH! from somewhere off the front starboard quarter. Caught up in the moment, he let go of the rail to adjust the binoculars, not so easy at night with so few lights visible outside. Whatever it was that had captivated him before it disappeared beyond the horizon had certainly not suggested the familiar grey and white of the dolphins, though.

Listening again for any sign of Kayden or Sadie, Jack cautiously edged his way along the bowsprit (fenced around with a tubular steel rail called a 'pulpit'). Edging his way to the front, where the rail dipped a little and leaning out slightly, at the same time, he happened to raise the binoculars in the hope of stealing another glance at the only other creature awake like him. His mysterious aquatic companion had, even from a distance, left the surface of the water flowing towards the boat churned by its spiral dance.

Just then, an off-shore wind happened to knock the *Jon T* sideways on its anchor and as Jack lost his footing with no time to cry out and tumbled into the inky waters, carried the sound of the splash far away. For a few seconds he floundered and tried to tread water, before feeling himself tugged under by the current.

And it was this sequence of events and the sound capsule swallowed up by the sea which caught the attention of a dolphin. One of the small pod which had played around them earlier, now she was resting in the warm sheltered pools, a mile or so from where Jack had fallen. Realising it would be too late to save the child by the time she could reach him, what she did instead sent a sonar message to someone or something else. Known to her as *the Messenger*, though twice as far away, he turned in the opposite direction, swift as an arrow fired from a bow. Diving deep below the waves, he resurfaced directly underneath the unconscious child, gently lifting him.

Seconds before, a strange calm had descended for Jack.

Was this how it felt to drown?

★ ★ ★

Moments before losing consciousness, metres below the surface, Jack had become aware of a powerful force churning

MOONTIDE

the water beneath him. Scooping up its precious human cargo and holding it safely in the space between its wings, the creature lifted, soaring out of the sea and into the air in one graceful arc.

He wasn't drowning then...

Jack was still unconscious when, sometime later, the creature drew in its wings and came to rest on an uninhabited island, where it set down the sleeping boy. At the same time, his rescuer had the presence of mind to roll Jack onto his stomach, before breathing a pile of dry sticks and dead leaves into a roaring fire.

Crisis averted, only then did it settle down beside him, sheltering him with its wing.

Within minutes, Jack stirred and with a series of convulsions, brought up the salty water he'd taken in since hitting the waves. Struggling to open his eyes as they smarted but feeling the reassuring warmth of the crackling fire and a comforting presence, he managed to sit up and lean against a rock, moving slightly away to get a better view of his protector.

He could see the creature now, its reclining body not nearly as long as the boat, though maybe two metres longer if you included the impressive tail. Jack's eyes widened as he took in the animal who carried him on (his, her or its?) powerful back. Soft and covered with a mixture of dense, silken fur and hairy tendrils, these gave way to scales at the edges of the wings. Another line of scales flowed the length of its back, starting just in front of the wings almost to the tip of its tail. Their iridescence caught the light of the moon as *the Messenger* shook himself *dog-like* to dislodge the last of the water soaking his coat.

Strange that at no time did Jack feel in fear – instinct had told him that the creature meant him no harm, its timely intervention prompted only by his tumble overboard. Besides, as Jack could now see when it turned to look at him, his deliverer had a friendly face, the large amber eyes smiling in relief as Jack plucked up the courage to speak

'Err… Sir… excuse me… do you speak English?'

'But of course!' chuckled the sea dragon

'I can speak many languages. But first, how's the breathing – have you got rid of all that sea water now? Quite an impressive tumble you had there, Jack.'

Odd, he didn't remember telling the creature his name but continued

'I thought I was going to drown but I feel strangely okay – *better than okay*!'

'Glad to hear it,' his rescuer replied 'We're not so very far from your boat – I thought I recognised it.

Humans aren't designed to live in the sea so if you feel strong enough to walk – just over there – We'll find you some water more suitable to drink. You won't find better, straight from a mountain stream…'

then laughing at Jack's sharp intake of breath 'Sorry, I was about to add… and *icy cold*!'

'Thank you!' Jack replied

'I mean for the water *and* for rescuing me. But how is it you know my name? And what's yours?'

'You're most welcome!' the beast replied 'My name is …………'

No good, the words made no sense to Jack, a mixture of bubbling, punctuated with some high-pitched sounds like the dolphins made. He could not for a moment have repeated or remembered it.

The dragon must have read Jack's helpless expression, as he turned and seemed to be smiling

'You did ask! I was teasing, it does n't exist in any human

language but translates roughly to *the Messenger*. It might become clearer why they call me that a little later, but still a bit formal. How about you call me *Finn* instead? That's a name given to me by a holy man a few hundred years ago: He fell into the sea whilst trying to catch a fish from an offshore lookout point and called me that when I retrieved him... once he was satisfied I wasn't going to eat him!'

'I'm glad you didn't want to eat me either, Finn. You saved my life and I've never met anything... Sorry, *anyone*... of your kind before'.

Jack felt Finn's sides shake as he chuckled again

'You don't surprise me – there are very few of us left. Don't be scared and if you're feeling a bit stronger, we need to crack on. I'd like to show you something and then return you before your Mum and Kayden wake'.

Jack was impressed

'How d'you know Kayden...?'

'I don't really, but there's a connection, you'll see in a moment.

First though, we should move over to the far side of those chalk cliffs across to the right. It'll help explain about my title, why they call me *the Messenger*. We could walk, but to save time, if you've got rid of all that surplus sea water and you'd like to scoot up onto my back again, flying will be safer and quicker: Best we avoid any more accidents tonight!'

Finn obligingly sat while Jack clambered onto his back. 'Hold tight now, won't take long.'

★ ★ ★

No sooner had they taken off than Finn was hovering, whilst he sussed out a suitable landing spot. Touchdown was graceful and no rush of brakes!

'If you'd like to take a seat on those rocks, our show can begin shortly. See that big empty space free of plants on the rock face just to your right?'

Jack nodded

'Let's pretend that is your local cinema screen. Keep your eyes focussed on the rock face. No questions for a few moments, just while I close my eyes and concentrate. Keep your eyes on that area... Ready?'

Jack nodded again and seconds later, could see flickering towards the centre, first white, then a rainbow of colours which swirled for a few seconds before spreading outwards, pixelating and settling into a picture.

Jack gasped as he gazed on the smiling face of a girl with deep golden skin, her light brown hair braided into neat corn rows. She carried in front of her a tray, taking it over to a large trestle table located in the shade of a palm tree. Setting it down with meticulous care, she was joined almost immediately by a man who was strangely familiar to Jack.

Tall with sandy blond hair and a bit of a beard, he came over and lifted one of the brightly coloured specimens for closer examination.

Jack exclaimed 'That's Mikey – Kayden's son Michael? I've not met him yet, but there's a photo of him and Kayden on the boat! You know Kayden through Mikey then?'

'He's actually helping in one of my favourite projects, Jack: a coral farm based in the Bahamas. You've heard of the Great Barrier Reef in Australia, right? Well, the work Mikey's doing will help re-establish parts of the Great Barrier Reef and other, less famous, coral reefs worldwide: Those worst affected by the activities of man during the last 200 years.

Did you know that the earth has existed for more than 4 billion years, humans for the last 315,000 of those years, yet almost *all* of the damage which now threatens our world has happened in the last 200 years, at least since the Industrial Revolution.'

'WOW... but how did Mikey get to be involved and meet you?'

Finn burst out laughing, momentarily distracted by the girl on the screen and Mikey, who was giggling as he saw the back of her T-shirt

'Look... he's only just noticed what it says.'

'But what's she carrying? Is it an animal... or a plant, I can't tell! Can we zoom in...'

Finn smiled indulgently

'I'm still working at this projection yet, but if you wait just a few more seconds, I'm sure Isabella – she's the girl with Michael – is going to oblige us and turn around.'

And the moment she turned, Jack laughed when he read

'SSSSSH... My Corals are sleeping!'

'Ah, I see now, the coral you were talking about. Why's Isabella walking around with it though, and why's Mikey taking a sample of the water in those trays?'

'Now for the exciting bit. They're testing the water temperature and quality before more baby corals arrive later. Just look at the variety of colours and shapes even in that one small tray! Just a few of the infinite varieties which exist in the world's oceans. Their next task will be to sort them into different groups. Some of them come from the deep ocean troughs where there's very little light penetration, but even miles beneath the waves, the world's coral cannot escape the effects of global warming.

In the wild, a difference of 1-2 degrees can make it too warm for the algae the coral feeds on, so if it stays like that, both the algae and the coral dies. I'm sure you've seen pictures of that whitish grey 'ghost coral' as it's called?'

Jack nodded

'I like watching TV programmes about the oceans, but it makes me sad. Kayden and I watched a series with Sir David Attenborough where it showed the impact our day-to-day lives are having on wild animals and their environments thousands of miles away … both land animals and sea creatures. He even got me the poster about it. But I'm sad that time is running out and now it will take a lot of people to stop the damage and make a difference. I hate that I can't do more about it. I did like the last programme in the series though and it made me feel that it may not be too late…'

Finn nodded

'Well, Michael (who I reckon you'll meet very soon) and Bella, are out there making a difference. He's already been out in the Bahamas for two months since completing his master's degree in Marine Biology and Bella is very much set on the same path. She idolises Michael, who's about to start his Doctorat in the next few weeks, whereas she's awaiting her results from her first degree. She'll be fine; I have it on good authority!

After a month's break, the two of them will be dotting between the coral farming venture and one of the other environmental protection and rebuilding projects worldwide, a few places where the clock is being turned back from the effects of global warming!

Michael, Bella and their colleagues are part of a mission to raise strong and healthy new corals: Those baby corals you saw in the tray and many others like them will help re-establish the Barrier Reef and some of the world's other coral reefs.

But Jack still needed to know

'How about Kayden though – you said you '*sort of* 'knew him?'

Finn didn't have much time left before Jack would be missed, but needed to answer before taking him back

MOONTIDE

'When he wasn't much older than you, Michael was travelling with his Dad. There they were, heading back to Miami from the Turks & Caicos Islands just the two of them on that same fine boat you fell from tonight. I can see you already love the boat almost as much as those two, though tonight you've learned a painful lesson about taking risks...'

Jack was nodding, ashamed for a moment

'To continue my story, Michael had a mishap of his own – a bit like you did tonight – and I was alerted to rescue him. Like you, he loved to sneak on deck and watch the dolphins in the day and the stars at night, pondering life on faraway planets. Whilst leaning out to try and get a better look at a Manatee through his binoculars, he just happened to go overboard and once he'd recovered, I showed him images of the plans for the conservation project he's now working on. Fourteen years ago, it was not much more than a brave idea in the minds of a few of the world's top scientific minds, but he knew from that moment that he wanted to study Marine Biology.'

Your distress call came from a dolphin, but on that occasion, it was a West-Indian manatee, the type Michael had been watching, the only type which can live both in fresh water *and* sea water. D'you know what a manatee is. (continuing as Jack nodded) Wonderful, peaceful creatures they are. Despite their size though, their skin is surprisingly delicate and they're also highly vulnerable to temperature changes.

It was only dusk when Michael fell overboard. Luckily, I managed to scoop him up and return him safely to the boat but it's possible Kayden may have got a glimpse of me when I returned his son. The light was poor though and I bet Kayden convinced himself he'd imagined what he saw!

I think the unexpected encounter with me and the rarity of seeing a whole group of manatees – an *aggregation* they call it, quite a sight as they don't live in herds – deepened Michael's interest in Marine creatures, both large and small. If you're interested, there's no reason you can't do work like his one day.

Plus, you're not tied to one project-there are many other ground-breaking environmental endeavours you can choose to work on, both on land and at sea. Another option might be one of the reclamation and re-foresting schemes in the Amazon. Very different work, so you might like to spend one month in the Bahamas and another elsewhere.

Choose your school subjects carefully and who knows where it may take you, especially when you've already got a family connection on this one! While Michael's there, you could keep up with him on video call, even spend a Summer out there when you're old enough to join him: How's that sound?

Down to business now. Have those pyjamas dried out yet and do they have a pocket? There's a tiny colourful pebble by your foot, one you can carry around to remind you of our meeting. It's from where the coral project is based, not these cold British waters of yours! You certainly have more colour back – open your mouth and say '*AAAH!*': All good, no trace of seawater in there from what I can see – God knows we've little enough without your swallowing half!'

Finn's face creased momentarily in a grin before turning serious again

'Now Jack, it really *is* time to head back: Kayden's going to be doing his checks anytime soon and my wings have dried out; I think we're ready to roll'.

Jack was reflecting on all that had happened in the last few hours.

'Thanks for everything, Finn… Will I ever see you again?'

The dragon smiled

'I like to think so, more likely, though, if you happen to get involved in one of the projects I was talking about, when you're a little older.

Please be careful on boats, though. You were lucky this time, and sheer coincidence that those dolphins you were friendly with put the word out while I was near enough to help. Now, time to climb aboard. Bury both your hands in my coat and wrap the strands around them. Last flight tonight, and this time, you won't get wet! Tug when you're ready and keep tight hold till I set you down.

Think of me as a helicopter – I'll circle and tell you exactly what to do. Your job is to follow my instructions, or I'll end up dropping you straight into the sea and we'll be back to square one!'

So, with Jack safely aboard, Finn rose once more into the air, sailing high above the cliffs, just below the edge of the clouds, before starting their descent.

As the *Jon T* came into view, they circled a final time and then glided in the general direction of the foredeck.

'I'll get as close as I can – once I tell you, use my back like a slide and my tail as a rope to lower yourself with – only let go once it's safe.'

All too soon, Finn gave the order and Jack was reluctantly sliding away from his comfortable seat between the wings and safely down the powerful back towards Finn's tail as they hovered less than 3 metres above the deck.

Using the tail like a rope Jack held on tight, before dropping the last metre or so onto the deck, rolling to cushion his landing.

By the time he looked up, his friend was soaring again into the sky

'Goodbye my friend and remember what I said.'

'Always!' As Jack reached the cockpit, he stopped, quieting his breath to listen for any sound. This time closing the hatch before securing the bolts on either side and fastening the brass hook, he made it back to his cabin just seconds before Kayden, with a big yawn, emerged from his cabin and padded upstairs onto the deck, scratching his head.

'Must have dreamt it!' Kayden said to himself, dismissing the strangest feeling, on waking, that he'd left the hatch unsecured.

'I'd best check the anchor first, then look in on Jack so I can settle for… (checking the saloon clock)… okay, a couple of hours, is that all! Must have overslept, best Sadie doesn't get to hear of it… not the best role-model for the youngster, but at least I was wrong about that hook on the hatch! Strange how that mug of Jack's ended up on deck, though. I'd swear Sadie refilled it hours after he went to sleep…'

By the time Kayden came back down, Jack was safely tucked up. Before closing his eyes though, he checked in his pocket for the pebble.'

★ ★ ★

Jack woke to Sadie's gently pulling at his arm

'Jack wake up I've been calling you for ages! Time to grab some breakfast. Here's some milk – couldn't find that mug of yours, sorry, but you'd best get dressed and do your teeth as soon as you can – Kayden's keen to leave soon!'

An hour later, they'd left the South coast behind and were making a good start en route to France. Jack was standing on the foredeck, harness safely clipped on over his lifejacket and his job right now, reporting to Kayden if he saw any ships of whatever size heading their way. For now, they were motor-sailing-sails and engine – to get some distance behind them before switching off to see how things went.

Even Sadie was excited and upbeat!

Over the next several hours, Kayden was happy with the progress and by late afternoon, they were anchoring just off Cap de la Hague and an hour later, were sitting tired and relaxed over a meal in the saloon when Kayden's phone rang.

'Hey, Mikey…!'

Kayden was delighted to hear from his son. 'Thanks for calling – Can we move on to FaceTime, if that's okay with you, there's something important and I wanted to tell you!

And 2 minutes later

'So, Sadie and Jack are here with me – Wave guys…' to an accompaniment of frantic waving all round and greetings called out between Sadie, Jack and Mikey.

'You've met Sadie a couple of times before on our video catchups, but I don't think you've met Jack, so here he is – to say he's excited to meet you is an understatement and you'll meet him for real in just a few days when you join us at La Rochelle.

'You bet, still on for that Dad, just as keen to meet Jack and Sadie and I'm hoping to spend a few days with you all on my favourite boat before I take the train down to see Maria in Aix. Apologies, Sadie, I'm forgetting you and Jack have n't met the others yet! My sister, the baby of the family, right now is on a gap year improving her French and my little brother, Joe has just started in his final year reading Physics at Edinburgh, but due home for Thanksgiving.

'I'll head South for a few days with Maria after I've visited with you, then fly back from Marseille. Funny how you can miss the cold working somewhere hot for weeks at a stretch – so I'm planning to take a week off and visit Mom in New Hampshire, meet up with Joe at the same time. Should have some snow by then!'

Jack was made up – Finn had been right about Mikey visiting!

'I heard… sorry, *thought,* you might be taking a break soon Mikey and I've got loads of questions!'

Just then, a face, familiar only to Jack, appeared beside Mikey, waving at the camera as she burst in

'Hi Guys, sorry to interrupt. I just got the ETA on our next arrivals, Mikey: We should be quiet for the next hour... so more than enough time to chat *and* get some lunch.'

She handed him a large mug of coffee.

And before he could stop himself, Jack had grabbed the tablet...

'BELLA! Tell me you're coming too? There's plenty of room and I want to hear how your baby corals are doing, A friend told me they've got an important job to do one day.'

Kayden was puzzled, but for now, looked at Sadie, shrugged and took another sip of his beer.

THE END

NOT MANY ELEPHANTS

Not many Elephants in Vermont

Prologue:

I was apprehensive.

My recently divorced cousin, Christian, had been keen for some time to get stuck into a volunteering project in some far-flung place, mainly to take his mind off splitting with his childhood sweetheart, Alison. They'd started dating at age 16, rented a flat by the time they were 20 and married just as they were turning 24 and expecting their son. Sixteen years on and it was a double whammy, with Chris turning 40 against a background of Ali packing her bags in the same week.

Surfing for ideas, he'd eventually settled on a project in South Africa, where he'd be in his element for four weeks, three volunteering in a game reserve, then a final week helping to look after elephants. A month ago, he'd dangled this last bit in front of me to tempt me to offload a fortnight of the precious leave I needed to use (or lose) by the year end. By then, my contract would be up and the plan was to open a small bookshop. I have to say that whilst I wasn't especially fussed by the first bit of his trip, the combo of subsidised flights (on a Cyber Monday B.O.G.O.F. deal) and having chance to care for baby elephants, was an almost irresistible lure.

But I passed; Chris wasn't tied to work as I was.

'Join us for the last 2 weeks?' he'd ventured, in a last-ditch gambit to avoid a whole month alone. Chris had enjoyed a variety of long-haul adventures and adored flying, unflustered by turbulence, short of a wing's dropping off.

Shame on me though; As the interfering cousin who'd urged

Chris to be brave and expand his horizons as a solo traveller, I could dish it out but couldn't really take it myself.

I'd been almost instantly put off by the 2 flights (or possibly 3 with the add-on?) plus the thought of slaving away on a money-making concern for 2 weeks to line the pockets of some uncaring commercial entity. Not for me those people paying upwards of £500 per night for butler-serviced rooms, returning from their game drives to sink cocktails on the terrace, while just 10 minutes down the road, kids living under the axles of abandoned wagons struggled to find enough to eat.

It really wasn't resonating with me and I used some feeble excuse of half-made plans to visit a friend.

It had been encouraging though, to see the smile on Chris' face as he flicked through his itinerary, sipping his last *flat white* on British soil for a month as we waited at Manchester for his flight to be called.

Half an hour later, I'm staring at his empty cup and unfinished cinnamon pastry, promising myself I'll leave it till tomorrow before sending a message: casual, upbeat and definitely NO hint of this being any sort of big deal for him.

Chris had at least 2 flights, followed by an hour – or was it two? – by Jeep.

Waking next morning, my mind turned to him again. Right now, he might still be on layover between the flights, but I'd quickly lost track: Time to bite the bullet anyway: He was bound to feel lonely and disoriented for a day or two till the mixed bag of British, German, Dutch and Americans connected and began to bond. I rushed to type a short friendly message, accidentally missing out the magic '**3**' as I typed in Chris's mail address.

NOT MANY ELEPHANTS

To: cjos@ ....
From: natbookworm@............
Date: 10th November
Time: 13.15
Subject: Adventures

Greetings from a cold and damp Derbyshire.

How's it going – are you there yet and how were the flights – did you get any sleep on the way over?

Oh and what about the elephants, have you seen many yet?

FaceTime me at the weekend, assuming you get time off for good behaviour. I've been tasked by Joyce to check you're not too skinny and see whether those dazzling white legs are getting any colour yet.

Not sure yet whether her interest is noble: I suspect she's got designs on a closer examination when you're back. Did I not tell you she's free again? I had hopes for that last guy she met on the new dating hub, but they only lasted 2 months. Thought that hair looked a funny colour...

Seriously though, don't let that put you off... and while you're out there, just say YES to everything that's not illegal.

Have fun, take care and don't get eaten by a lion!

Love,

Nat

X

PS Sneaked into Boots while you were in the loo and grabbed some condoms just in case... left them in the side pocket of your bag, forgot to mention, sorry...

MOONTIDE

To: natbookworm@............
From: cjos@............
Date: 10th November
Time: 07.05
Subject: **Adventures**

Hi back,

Thought I heard a beep earlier!

On my second coffee here, about to grab a harness and hang off the side of an icy building as soon as they call me. Having to speed-read this so I'll finish it later if I'm called…

Flight time Atlanta – Manchester was just over 2 hours… plus another two for the drive to Vermont, though Dad's old Bronco eats the miles.

Puzzled though, were you expecting a delay?

And *Sleep?* I don't usually sleep on these short flights, power-napping's not my thing.

Elephants – Seriously, *did I read that correctly?* I wasn't expecting to see elephants in Vermont, especially in November: Right now, they'll be gearing up for the ski-season (the Mountain Resort that is, not the elephants) with barely two weeks left to Thanksgiving!

And you can forget anything you've read about Hannibal; The Dude clearly had some way with elephants to be able to coax them up over the Alps as he did: Ordinarily, they wouldn't like the snow, they'd slide around too much.

If they were anywhere up here though, I'm guessing they'd do better just off the Mountain road, somewhere near the *Von Trapp Family Lodge*; nice and flat for the cross-country lovers, plenty of guests around to give them treats and sing to keep them calm.

Sorry, have to dash, catch you later or else at the site review meeting tomorrow!

Best,

CJ

To: natbookworm@............

From: cjos@............

Date: 10th November

Time: 10.30

Subject: **Adventures huh?**

Hi again,

Back in the site office now and trying to find the coffee – bear with me while I read on. Best I try and reply while it's brewing... Likely I'll get paged again anytime.

What's this about *time off for good behaviour*? Come to think of it, that, together with the stuff about *elephants*... and *lions*

(Where exactly do the lions come in? Trust they're nowhere near the elephants?)

plus that PS just made my blood run cold.

– So, since I'm pretty sure you're not my cousin Maisie with the revised plans from our Burlington office, do you mind if I pause for a moment to enquire

WHO EXACTLY IS THIS?

and secondly

You put WHAT in my luggage?

Best,

CJ

NOT MANY ELEPHANTS

To: cjos3@............

From: natbookworm@............

Date: 10th November

Time: 16.30

Subject: **Adventures** – and Sorry!

Hi Chris,

SO Sorry! I sent you a message earlier but looks like I misdirected it, so I'm pasting it right here...

I've just terrified a complete stranger somewhere in the USA – somewhere *cold* I should add-with my prattling on about elephants and lions (I'm putting a read-receipt on all my outgoing mail to you from here in, avoids any more cockups...)

Subject: **Adventures**

Greetings from a cold and damp Derbyshire.

How's it going – are you there yet and how were the flights – did you get any sleep on the way over?

Oh and what about the elephants, have you seen many yet?

FaceTime me at the weekend, assuming you get time off for good behaviour. I've been tasked by Joyce to check you're not too skinny and see whether those dazzling white legs are getting any colour yet.

Not sure yet whether her interest is noble: I suspect she's got designs on a closer examination when you're back. Did I not tell you she's free again? I had hopes for that last guy she met on the new dating hub, but they only lasted 2 months. Thought that hair looked a funny colour ...

Seriously though, don't let that put you off ...and while you're out there, just say YES to everything that's not illegal.

Have fun, take care and don't get eaten by a lion!

Love,

Nat

X

PS Sneaked into Boots while you were in the loo and grabbed some condoms just in case... left them in the side pocket of your bag, forgot to mention, sorry …

Speak soon anyway

More love

Nat

X

To: cjos@............

From: natbookworm@.............

Date: 10th November

Time: 17.45

Subject: **Monumental Cock-up**

Hi Mr.......?

Is Mr, okay? I realise I don't know who I'm talking to here... for all I know you might be Doctor, or Reverend, or Professor ...*please not Reverend though*, I'll die of shame.

At the risk of annoying you further, please may I have a surname or a pseudonym, something/anything I can call you by for the time it takes me to apologise tonight – I'm going redder and redder typing this, I know you can't *see* me, that's not the point.

Before I close and await your reply with a name (real or alias) I'm including a bit below about me, which I hope will reassure you no harm was intended ....

Anyway, Hi (again). My proper name is *Natalie Gertrude Margarita O'Sullivan* though I'm known as 'Nat'.

[You're the first person I've told in ages about the *Gertrude*, Dad's Great Aunt, beautifully eccentric and glamorous, never married. The *Margarita* is from Margarita Island, where my parents went on Honeymoon... enough said!) and before you start worrying that I'm trying to steal your identity or working for the IRS or the CIA, I'm no-one important, just a girl with aspirations to start a Bookshop (hence the *bookworm*, it's not a codename or anything... only just realised how *bookworm* sounds like a hacker in one of those Scandi thrillers)].

So, if my *bookworm* hasn't made things worse, I didn't mean you any harm and I'm just a bookstore worker from Bakewell in

Derbyshire. My passport number (British, obviously) is .... just in case you want to check me out on *Accuity* or anything... but I promise you'll be rid of me by tomorrow and I'll do my best not to cause you any more trouble if you'd just be so kind to confirm your name, while I finish explaining.

(Happy to explain more about my mistake when/if you reply.)

Sorry

Kind Regards

Nat

PS I should add so far as relevant: Passport issued in Liverpool on 4 January 2021 – *Sod it – why would you believe me now? I'm attaching a copy for your further reassurance]*

NOT MANY ELEPHANTS

To: natbookworm@.................
From: cjos@ ....
Date@10th November
Time: 17.40
Subject: **Explains a lot**

Hi Nat,

(is it Nat or do you expect Natalie from a stranger? I totally get that it's not *Gertrude* nor *Margarita*.

And *O'Sullivan,* huh? (Passport not necessary, nice photo).

Now you've identified yourself, I'm guessing the surname is partly to blame; I'm one too *(an O'Sullivan, that is.* Carlton Joseph O'Sullivan II if I'm reciprocating – *Mister*'s fine by the way, but no need…).

Well Ms *Natalie Gertrude Margarita O'Sullivan,* you certainly livened up an uneventful day, that's aside from the site inspection bit. My job's to decide what strengthening should be done for a building – part renovation, part new-build, a ski-lodge basically, but all clinging to a hillside and I don't particularly do heights (who does?!).

The distraction certainly took my mind off it for a while, anyway, so thanks for that at least.

I'd say you're forgiven, but I'm keen to read the rest of your apology first.

Best,

CJ

(a.k.a. Carlton etc as above).

PS what time is it there? I'm thinking you may not see this till tomorrow.

MOONTIDE

To: cjos@..........

From: natbookworm@...........

Date: 10th November

Time: 23.47

Subject: **Monumental Cock-up – part 2 of 2**

Hi Carlton,

Still up… just!

Debating whether to call you 'CJ' in case it's reserved for friends? You'll understand I'm playing safe, after last time!)

Thanks for yours and as should now be indicated above, as yours pinged in I think it was 10.40 pm, so makes us five hours apart.

Early start tomorrow, but I wanted to finish my explanation and apology when I hit you by mistake (Sorry again). Message was meant for my cousin, Chris (another O'Sullivan) currently chasing elephants in South Africa, first holiday since splitting with his soulmate. They were love's young dream, but I'm mindful at some point Chris will be over it and looking to move on (hence my sneaking the articles mentioned into his bag. I'm not involved in Family Planning or anything, it was a spontaneous gesture to protect him in a different world from the one where he and Ali took up together).

So, nothing sneaked in yours, rest assured.

I'm dying here… never crossed my mind till now how it might look if he got searched at Customs! (Or for that matter if someone else received my mail destined for Chris – FECK, face glowing again!).

Anyway, I can see now why my mail landed in your box. All to do with missing out one tiny little '3' – identical mail addresses, except for his having that pesky little '3' tucked in there. (Imagine that! Don't you find it fascinating; One single, ordinary numeral sneaked in or missed out and look at all the complications it can cause!)

Sorry again and I'd say it was great to chat with you – What an interesting job you have and how fabulous that your work sends you to a ski resort!

I love ski-ing and don't get to go very often whereas my friend in New Hampshire has two resorts within easy driving distance and a ski pass each season! Anca always rubs it in that there's normally a good snowfall by *Thanksgiving*. I've been to visit once but I did just manage to miss both Thanksgiving and the *Foliage:* Been intending to go back each year since but either money or time has forced me to postpone.

(There's another thing I envy you for – how come you get to have Thanksgiving? And sold it to me the moment she described it as 'like Christmas without the commercial side').

Anyway, it's been nice knowing you for a short time (albeit under a mistake!) and here I am making this worse, taking up far too much time with my rabbiting ... YIKES! My own as yours, alarm goes off in 6 hours!

So, I'll sign out with

Bye for now Carlton and thanks a million for your gracious understanding,

KR

Nat.

MOONTIDE

To: natbookworm@...........

From: cjos@............

Date: 10th November

Time: 22.37

Subject: **Monumental Cock- up – 3 of 2, I guess?**

Hi Nat,

Thanksgiving – You have heard of the *Pilgrim Fathers*, and *the Mayflower*, right?

If not, happy to expand but I'll assume that was a joke? I'm not surprised you'd like a piece of it, it is wonderful and to honour those early settlers, we usually return home for a big family gathering. Before we eat though, we go around the table giving thanks, each person singling out a particular something they're thankful for before we get stuck into the food. Just a wonderful day full of Gratitude and food is my take on it.

Ski-ing – Yes indeed, snow's falling as I write this – I just lifted the curtain to check before I press send and head out for some (glacial) air.

The snow ploughs are at it right now, the slopes around Mount Mansfield are floodlit for night-ski-ing: Romantic, sure, but extra layers needed!

My work here should stop in about four days but I'm staying on for Thanksgiving. Brought my boots up with me but I've hired skis – bindings nice and loose for now, can't wait to get them on!

Rabbiting – what a quaint turn of phrase!

If you can find any time to *rabbit* a little more tomorrow (since

it's the wee small hours out there by now) I'll read it after work.
CJ

PS 'CJ' is fine, not even my Mom calls me Carlton, unless she's mad with me. Stop agonising over these things, again so *British*.

Look, consider we're 'friends' if that simplifies communication?

Perhaps we'll meet one day: Hoping to get a trip to London (work again) in the Spring – We could meet for coffee if the drive's not too far.

PPS not *Reverend*.

To: cjos@................
From: natbookworm@..............
Date: 11th November
Time: 16.58
Subject: **Pissed!**

Hi Carlton,

I was enjoying our correspondence till you went and upset me, hence my sitting on this for a few hours before sending.

Note the title: I'm using the American sense of the word on this occasion. Still at work, I don't want any misunderstandings …

You didn't read mine properly, did you? *Bakewell* is in the Peak District, God's own country, a zillion miles from London in every sense. Like many Americans, you seem to think that life in 'England' revolves around London and the rest of us are out in the sticks.

London's about 200 miles away, the Midlands are nice and balanced as the location would suggest, our main job here being to keep the peace between the North and South; we've done it successfully for centuries now – roughly since the time of King Alfred.

Best,

Nat

PS Did you miss me… *just a little?*

NOT MANY ELEPHANTS

From: cjos@...............
To: natbookworm@................
Date: 11th November
Time: 12.32
Subject: **My goof this time**

Dear Nat,

I get it. You're annoyed with me for not reading yours properly, not drunk yet!

(In mitigation, I was adjusting my harness ready to abseil down a cliff face, currently covered in snow, snow on top of *ice)*

Anyways, I hope you'll forgive me, and I sense absolution is more likely if I reply soonest – I was really starting to enjoy our exchanges.

That's two women I've upset in one day... Other was Mom, when I told her I may not be heading over for Thanksgiving.

Might have to reconsider... meanwhile, what can I do to say I'm sorry for having you pegged as a 'Londoner'? Not flowers, I'm sensing: You might be tempted to mistreat them; put them straight in the trash; or chop their heads off. Either way, I can't take the risk.

How can I convince you to excuse me? I'm thinking a voucher for a restaurant somewhere near you on the evening of Thursday 27th .... that's Thanksgiving by the way.

I'll set myself a task to find a place somewhere near, unless you have a favourite. Throw me a fish here, Nat – What's your thing – traditional, Curries, Thai...? I don't think Sushi particularly screams 'Thanksgiving', but hey, if that's what you want, I'll run with it.

Perhaps we could FaceTime if I can time my Thanksgiving lunch to around 3.00pm – fit in with when you're having dinner?

Right now, I need to get back on site – getting distracted, your fault again, reminding me about Thanksgiving!

Sorry again,

CJ

PS Yes, I did (Miss hearing from you earlier)

NOT MANY ELEPHANTS

To: cjos@....................
From: natbookworm@.................
Date: 11th November
Time: 18:12
Subject: **Absolution**

Think you can buy me with food do you, CJ?

You're getting to know me already! Sushi, though... *seriously?*

Consider yourself forgiven: I love the idea of going out to eat on Thanksgiving, but if it's not too presumptuous, do you mind if I take a 'friend'?

Sorry to be so cheeky, but with my lonely table for 1, I'm scared they'll assume I'm a prostitute.

Nat

x

To: natbookworm@..................

From: cjos@...............

Date: 11th November

Time: 13:32

Subject: ***Is that a Kiss or does my screen need cleaning?***

Hi Nat,

I just called *The Square*. Any good? Hoping it's okay as I reserved a table for you, 8.00pm.

Trying to impress you with my geography this time – if *Waze* is correct, it shouldn't be more than a few miles, menu sounds promising!

Table for 2 in view of your (understandable) concern.

Think I've earned a favour in return: Pray for me, I'm about to ring Mom and postpone my visit to Keene, in my defence there's already a good depth of packed powder here – I did a run earlier and it's all coming back. Hoping the matriarch will understand as she taught me to ski in the first place!

CJ x

PS I'm forgetting – Keene's just down the road but over the state line into New Hampshire... can't be far from your friend, surely?

Did you ever see 'Jumanji?'

NOT MANY ELEPHANTS

To: cjos@....................
From: natbookworm@.................
Date: 11th November
Time: 20:05
Subject: **Change of Plan**

Hi CJ

Do cows eat grass... Do you think I was dragged up?
OF COURSE I'VE SEEN JUMANJI!

Just to impress you... I've also been to Keene – I was staying with my friend Anca, just South of Concord. Even took a selfie in the main square where they filmed those scenes of the Rampaging CGI animals!

Hope you don't mind but I'm cancelling the booking at *The Square*: *Postponing*, I should say, just putting it on ice if that's okay with you? I've been reminded I've still got some paid holiday left from the job I'm leaving at the end of the year, so I've decided to take a week's break while the going's good.

My best friend Joyce works in town at a travel agency called *Where Next?* Another friend of ours is working in Rome. If the flights work out, the 3 of us can spend a few days drinking wine and stuffing pasta in the Eternal City before Lou's packed off home: she's just round the corner from the Trevi fountain.

I'm still keen to FaceTime at same time on Thursday 27th – hopefully from a trattoria on the Piazza Navona if it's not too full of tourists! Joyce got us both such a good deal on our flights earlier this year, we're hoping to repeat.

Nat

x

MOONTIDE

To: cjos@..............

From: natbookworm@...................

Date: 12th November

Time: 09.58

Subject: **Pissed again**

SOD IT!

Rome's off.

Sodding deals have all gone, in fact all the sodding flights around the times/ days I wanted have gone!

Back to square one… damn, blast… feck the lot of them!

Nat

PS x

NOT MANY ELEPHANTS

To: cjos@..............
From: natbookworm@................
Date: 12th November
Time: 10:01
Subject: **Same**

Sincere apologies CJ, I should have taken a few deep breaths before applying finger to keyboard.

Are we still speaking?

Conscious you Americans seem far more bothered by language than we are here. Please don't be alarmed though, I'll be back to my normal self later.

Can we scratch my last and just go back to plan 'A', Please? – Really looking forward to our Thanksgiving meal on 27th (Joyce is too – she's my + *1*, so you'll get to 'meet' her too, all makes the world a little bit smaller!

Can't apologise enough for my language, I did once lose £23.50 (more than 2 weeks pocket money for a sixth former at the time) when we set up a charity swear box at school: That week, I remember the girls' side collecting far more than the boys, but at 25p a bad word, I certainly held my own for Lower VI B... We trounced the others and as the best contributor, it was my reward to present the cheque to Sister Mary – Dolores at the convent.

When I knocked to present it, I was deliberately economical with what I said about our year's *fund-raising initiative*. Didn't I blush down to my toes when it turned out she already knew the full story from her nephew. 'Robert' just happened to be doing a few weeks teacher training at our school. How come I never suspected they were connected? Sister D is cool, lovely lady. What a relief I didn't say that most of the class thought our new Mr Philbin was a bit of alright: Figures now, he took us for

Scripture. Those shoulder length curls and beard gave him a bit of a biblical look!

Nat

X

NOT MANY ELEPHANTS

To: natbookworm@..................
From: info@wherenext................
Date: 12th November
Time: 11.05
Subject: **Fairy Godfocker?**

Hi Nat,

Are you sitting down?

One of our busiest days, I've been in since 7.30 this morning so I can leave early.

Not long after I arrived, I got an interesting call from some bloke named CJ.

You never told me you had a cousin in the US? I've only known you, what, 25 years? I don't just know your family. I know the name of your first pet... the first boy you snogged at school ...bank security PIN.... *even your bra size*, but this was a new one on me.

Suppose I'll have to believe you for now as he did say CJ O 'SULLIVAN, though I don't recall your Dad having any brothers! What a voice too, I was tempted to record him. (said he was calling from Keene, New Hampshire...and yet, I caught a hint of a Southern drawl...)

So, there we have it; Not just a mysterious, hitherto-unspoken -of cousin but a cousin who's prepared to stump up Thanksgiving prices for return flights to Boston – Logan with Virgin!

Does the guy ever sleep? He sounded wide awake, considering the time difference.

Flights all booked, then!

Completely forgot to discuss accommodation, though I imagine you'll want to speak to Anca and Holly first?

Word though, should you need it. Expect to pay a lot more than usual. Anything affordable will already have been snapped up, though I'm sure your *cousin* will sub you... if he is your cousin? I'm still having serious doubts despite the name... just from Googling there are quite a few O' Sullivans on the East coast, just counting New Hampshire, Connecticut and Vermont!

For the booking, I just worked on the parameters you gave me yesterday, hoping that's still okay... let's see now

"Earliest to fly Out Tuesday 23rd, Returning no later than Sunday 5th"

is what I wrote, still got the post-it here.

On that basis, CJ insisted I go ahead and book it! I'll keep hold of the tickets here till tomorrow – assuming we're still on for the *Dog & Duck* at 6.30.

Let me know if not

Joyce

XX

PS Did I not mention...BUSINESS CLASS!

Happy to go in your place if booking doesn't suit.

NOT MANY ELEPHANTS

To: cjos@............

From: natbookworm@...............

Date: 12th November

Time: 12. 15

Subject: **Thanking you**

Hi CJ,

You'll just be getting up, so I'll keep it short.

Joyce has been in touch.

I don't know what to say other than it's the kindest thing anyone has ever done for me, Thank you!

Nat

X+X

PS If, as I'm assuming, you've got an early start on top of your nocturnal calls to my best friend, you'll be ready for bed by lunchtime! Your job sounds dangerous, so I need you to promise me you'll be extra careful today (heights/ harnesses and any risky stuff)?

To: cjos@.............

From: info@wherenext..........

Date: 12th November

Time: 12. 52

Subject: **Just checking**

Hi CJ,

Thanks for your call earlier and your booking. A pleasure to talk to you and Nat is abnormally silent today, overwhelmed by your surprise.

I quite forgot to mention, though: Accommodation – do you have that covered? If she needs somewhere, I'll get on it PDQ: Neither of us can get hold of our friend Anca who lives in Concord, I suspect she's gone to Hawaii as she was threatening it when we spoke earlier this year.

No reason to forewarn either of us when she wasn't expecting visitors.

Thanks and Regards

Joyce

PS Nat mentioned about *The Square*. Can I snaffle your booking? – A really good choice and I'll gladly reimburse anything you've paid up front. I've grown to like this idea of FaceTiming and stealing a few minutes of your Thanksgiving.

Don't have to prepare a speech or anything, do I?

NOT MANY ELEPHANTS

To: info@wherenext..............

From: mos@doric...............

Date: 14th November

Time: 18:44

Subject: **All Covered!**

Hi Joyce,

Sorry for the delay in replying to yours, been finishing up a few things before I drove down to Mom's. In 2 days, I'll be heading South to collect something we'll need for Thanksgiving, but she'd promised that if I could get here tonight before 7.00pm, she'll clear her diary for the whole of tomorrow to ski.

Mount Sunapee's handy for my flight from Manchester (New Hampshire, that is!). I'm off to Atlanta the following morning, one hour's drive will do nicely.

Before I forget though, would you let Nat know I'll have my hands full for a few days, though I'll be back sometime on 24th in time to collect her.

To answer your concerns:

Accommodation – got it covered.

Restaurant – Booking (for 2, in view of Nat's concern) left exactly as it was and fully funded – my gift for all your help last minute – no need to take any money unless you think there's a chance you and your +1 are going to eat your way through more than my pre-authorised limit of £150.00?

Hope you don't mind but I've made a few suggestions the staff can run by you…we could link up soon after you arrive!

One last thing – Can I suggest storing this mail address – Mom's company one – Nat will likely be based here for her first couple of nights.

Looking forward to putting a face to the voice next time we talk,

Best,

CJ

To: natbookworm@...............

From: mos@doric..............

Date: 14th November

Time: 19: 08

Subject: **Disappearing**

Hey there,

Sorry so late and we missed tonight, Joyce can explain, she was my priority(!).

Seriously, she'll fill you in.

I'll be down in Atlanta for a week or so: Dad's down there, it's where I grew up and still the hub of our family business – Architecture. My Dad's a practical man, so he heads up the Civil Engineering side of the practice, whereas Mom, a thousand miles away up here in Keene – is our hot shot on design and aesthetics. Not together now (in any sense) but lucky for us all, they still get along fine.

Bet you're wondering exactly where I fit in?

Most of the time, I suppose I'm more the 'gopher' and I don't mind flying and spreading myself between Atlanta and Keene while I try to absorb whatever I can from Mom, Dad and my star elder brother, Mark.

I'm hoping all this will eventually make me useful to the clients, in time for whenever our parents retire!

Plan now is to get some serious ski-ing time in with Mom tomorrow (Dad prefers cross-country, whereas Mark's a born-again snowboarder these last few years!).

I'll struggle to keep up with Mum till it comes back to me – she's an expert skier and still has way more stamina! Be good to get some quality time, just me and her, our last chance this year.

Talking of which, expecting my popularity to rocket when I return for Thanksgiving with one of her favourite Atlanta exports!

If you send me a message in the morning, I'll be able to see it tomorrow night – flight not till 3.00pm.

CJ

Xx

NOT MANY ELEPHANTS

To: GinaB@skininja..............

From: natbookworm@...............

Date: 15th November

Time: 09:20

Subject: **Help – Nothing fits!**

Hi, Gina

Joyce's mate Nat, glad I still have you stored – still at the shop?

Off ski-ing in a week, USA, it's been 2 years since I skied and I need to stock up on base layer tops, plus some more trousers, unless I lose half a stone very quickly: Dark pants with some cushioning to absorb all the bumps when I fall.

Any offers right now?

A reply before 12.00 would be great, I'll come over at lunchtime if you can see possibilities.

Nat

(Natalie O 'Sullivan)

MOONTIDE

To: natbookworm………….
From: GinaB@Skininja………….
Cc: Gina@DLSports………….
Date: 15th November
Time: 10.11
Subject: **Stop worrying**

Hi Nat,

Nice to hear from you! Still working for Donna but replying from my own mail as only due in at 12.00 today (lunch cover!).

I remember you trying those pants; frighteningly snug, not at all surprised you want something with a bit more room left to eat!

Some amazing offers on right now to make room for more new stock in December. There's a pair of luminous yellow pants you have to rule out before settling on anything plain. Plus bright is safer… no bad thing in a whiteout, right?!

I'll look out 2 or 3 other options as a default, next size up from your black ones, but seriously, when the yellow ones came in, it was like a scene from Cinderella.

What happened was Donna pulled up not long after the delivery guy left, to find the front door blocked by a pile of unsorted deliveries. Lucky she was in a good mood. The whole lot was where it was dumped while me, Lucy and Yaz were all huddled in the changing area, seeing if the yellow ones fitted any of us. If they'd been just a little bit looser and longer, they'd be off to Austria with me in 3 weeks!

Before I go though, have you thought about goggles – North East, right, with your friend? Assuming it's New England again, you're best with a tint that's either yellow, pink or orange – don't even think of taking those polarised shades you got for Spain, might look cool but you'll be lucky to see your hand in front of your face!

Drift over when you can and I'll shut you in the dressing room with coffee and a pile of stuff to try.

Gina

X

MOONTIDE

To: natbookworm@.............
From: GinaB@skininja............
Date: 15th November
Time: 14:37
Subject: **Lucky You!**

Hi Nat

Hoping your trip's shaping up nicely, told you those yellow pants would be perfect, didn't I? D'you realise you've saved over £130 between those and the goggles alone – easier than sunglasses where you're going.

Attached is my list of what you picked out: Any mistakes, tell me next 15 mins, after which I'll bag everything up bar the goggles. That way, you can squeeze it all into your travel bag – just pay when you collect them tomorrow. I'm designing the pack for quick-release in case you get searched at the Airport!

Thanks again for shopping with us –as you've hit the magic £200, you'll get a VIP discount card valid for the next 12 months.

Gina

X

P S Donna's covering from 2.00, so if I miss you have a great time, Yaz and I are off to Austria start of December before the 11th hour Christmas push.

NOT MANY ELEPHANTS

To: natbookworm@..............
From: info@wherenext...............
Date: 15th November
Time: 17:28
Subject: **Did you get sorted?**

Wanted to check before I lock up.

Did you get what you needed, *clothes-wise*?

Still got some 'teabags' left from Canada last year if you want them: Great ski-ing though proper cold and still not sure why they do different shaped warmers for hands and feet …they just need to be WARM!

I'll bring what I've got to the Pub on Friday with your tickets… never hurts to be prepared!

J

XX

To: cjos@.....................
From: natbookworm@.....................
Date: 15th November
Time: 22:38
Subject: **Just Hello**

Hi CJ,

I know you're wrapped up in things for a few days – no reply needed.

Picked up some more ski-ing gear today. You won't miss me on the slopes – I look like a class of pre-schoolers have attacked me with highlighter pen! At least my jacket is black ….

Can't get my head round it now… how close we are to meeting and all because of one tiny cock-up!

Starting to seem real now, so excluding tonight, let's see … 1, 2… 7 more sleeps!!

One week left at work then I'm finished and ready to take up my own lease. Planning to open in January but not signed yet, should just be time before New Year to get cracking on the painting and shelves. Dad's promised to help!

Nat

XX

NOT MANY ELEPHANTS

To: cjos3@.............

From: natbookworm@...............

Date: 16th November

Time: 10:58

Subject: **Something interesting came up ...**

Hope you're keeping those elephants in check?

Just back from meet up with Joyce at the Dog and Duck... food's still good, had the sausages tonight.

Now for the interesting bit: You'll recall my cock-up when I sent message destined for you to a stranger, right?

Since then, we – CJ and I – have become friends and – long story short

HE SKIS!

Which might explain why I'm off in one week's time to stay in the USA, just an hour or so from where Anca and Holly live.

Joyce is running me to Manchester for my flight and I'll see you the week before Christmas. Will send you a snow report once I'm there – your turn to be envious!

Nat

X

MOONTIDE

To: natbookworm@..............

From: info@wherenext...............

Date: 17th November

Time: 17:28

Subject: **Pub at 6.00?**

I'll be early, so I'll order 2 of the Sausages and mash just in case Jeff and the rugby crowd come up.

Kisses

J

To: info@wherenext...............

From: natbookworm@..............

Date: 17th November

Time: 17:34

Subject: **Pub at 6.15**

Give me ten minutes yet.

Our last Friday for a week or two, so we'll say my shout tonight.

Yours when I'm back…

Nat

X

NOT MANY ELEPHANTS

24 November

One tiny patch of turbulence mid-way, but I barely noticed as by then, I'd sank 2 mini bottles of Rioja.

My flight touched down at Boston sometime before 5.00 pm. I'd been up for almost 17 hours, but the tiredness starting to kick in was trumped by the excitement. Even the weather was playing its part. I'd boarded just before 10.30 am in a dark and drizzly Manchester but just prior to landing at Logan, had vistas of snow-capped fields as the First Officer started our approach and for the next twenty minutes, we were treated to a spectacular scene of a landscape dusted white and gold by the late afternoon sun.

Joining the queue for Immigration, the usual polite interrogation, then moments later, there I am wrangling my big squashy bag off the conveyor!

Another 10 mins and I'm anxiously scanning the Arrivals lounge for any sign of a man who could – at the furthest stretch of my imagination – be CJ. The only photo he'd scanned when mailing me was a bit blurry and I hadn't wanted to offend again quite so quickly by demanding another!

I'd been one of the last passengers to get my bag and 15 minutes later, the area was already starting to thin out, anxious glances turning one by one to smiles and shrieks, as returning loved ones were scooped in close for their first hugs in months, before being escorted away.

I'm still not seeing any likely contenders for CJ though, as I push my trolley, thankful for a prop: Most of the men left waiting were either the wrong side of 70 or else, under 30.

By now, I was starting to wonder if CJ had catfished me...

Stupid thought! I calmed down for just a few seconds before a second, more chilling possibility gripped me

– He must have been rushing and, tight for time, had veered off the icy road on the way to pick me up: Right now, he'd be lying unconscious in some State Hospital as the Medics applied the defibrillator... *Oh my God!*

Whilst my brain continued to wrap itself around one nihilistic thought after another, I'd completely missed the tall, elegant woman in the suede boots and fake fur duffel coat.

She'd stopped just yards away, a small boy in tow. Smiling sheepishly, she crouched down almost to the same level as the child, pinning shoulder length hair behind her ear before diving into a voluminous bag, from which her charge extracted a crumpled roll of white paper. This they unrolled before proudly raising it in a cascade of glitter, one each end so it sloped left to right as the woman straightened up.

WELCOME NATALIE!

Someone had gone to the trouble of colouring and cutting out some hearts and stars, before sticking them onto the printed banner... even a few elephants, one not quite holding as it came adrift and fluttered over towards me.

I picked it up, smiling at the child

'I think he belongs to you?'

Smoothing her jeans, the woman broke into a warm smile as, oblivious to the appreciative glances from some of the onlookers, she moved forward to offer a hug.

'It is *Nat,* isn't it?' As she thrust out a hand to squeeze mine

'Thank Heaven...*Marlee,* Marlee O'Sullivan, that is, CJ's Mom and this is my grandson, Matty.

Come say 'Hi' to our guest, she's flown a long, long way to meet you and Daddy. I'm sure she'll help us roll your banner back up.

I bent down just a little as I waited for him to approach, slight hesitation before he launched himself towards me, almost knocking me over in his quest to do a proper job , so my wobbles had him giggling.

'Now, if you would n't mind taking his hand while I try to retrieve my parking ticket, we'll go rescue the car. CJ had planned to collect you himself but he's currently with his brother in Concord, who right now is getting plastered in Copley...'

'He's *what?*'

I didn't realise I'd spoken out loud... but luckily it turned out to be a false alarm, another of those Anglo-American linguistic differences – as soon as Marlee caught on, she looked aghast and started laughing

'Sorry about that Nat – Two nations separated by a common language, huh? It's Mark's fault, my elder son. He's mad keen on the snowboarding, unlike CJ and I. CJ's unhurt, just handholding while Mark's leg is put in plaster. They'll stay in Stowe tonight and hopefully be down tomorrow.

Just us three – you, me and Matty – till then. We can chat as we drive up, that's if you're not too tired. I'm relieved to hear you're into ski-ing, not boarding. You should see them all jumping off at the top of Mount Mansfield, into the fog...!'

Another half hour by the time we'd rescued Marlee's Lexus – I was relieved to see just a little bit of clutter in the back; rolled up plans in a cluster of labelled tubes, a portfolio case lying open, pushed across to accommodate a hastily – fitted child seat for Matty; I noticed some sketches I could only assume might have something to do with the building CJ was working on in Stowe.

★ ★ ★

We'd soon left Boston behind us and purring up the interstate without the constant stop-starting, I may have drifted for a matter of minutes when I was suddenly aware of a much quieter snow-capped landscape. Matty was fast asleep, Marlee chatting as we headed North

'I'll be quiet if you want to snooze, but if you can fight it till we get back and you've had some supper, I promise you'll acclimatise better!'

It wasn't the effort I'd thought to stay awake as Marlee chatted away, with gaps when she checked her route.

'I still don't trust the sat nav!' she grinned, 'not that I'm so great at navigating …'

8.45pm now and I was glad I'd adjusted my watch while waiting for my bag, avoids waking up in the early hours looking for the loo with one eye open and assuming it was time to get up! Unlike Joyce, I've only flown across the Atlantic a few times and it makes me feel a bit weird for a day or so.

Now I thought about it, I was glad I'd have chance to recover, get used to my surroundings and focus entirely on offering whatever help I could to Marlee with the food preparations or entertaining Matty before CJ arrived and Thanksgiving was upon us.

Another two hours and we swung into a generous driveway, which curled around in front of a 2-storey white painted garrison-colonial style house: One with a porch that wrapped around the front and side, plus something I'd always wanted: a swing seat! So this house was home for tonight and possibly tomorrow, that would do nicely!

A small sign half-covered in snow hung just under the porch where it faced the roadway

Doric Associates

O'Sullivan

While Marlee was heating the soup she'd made for supper, she pointed out where I'd be sleeping.

'Up the stairs, second right. Door on the left of the room is for the ensuite, other connects with the adjoining room, CJs. I keep the connecting door locked but key is on your side!

NOT MANY ELEPHANTS

An hour later, Matty was in bed and Marlee and I were having seconds of the delicious soup. After we'd loaded the dishwasher, we retired to the den just off the kitchen, where we sat on opposite ends of the sofa, sipping hot chocolate and brandy in front of the log burner.

'Is it torture staying awake?' Marlee laughed, impressed I'd held up till now as she packed me off to bed with a hug and a 'See you tomorrow – you're bound to wake up early but if you don't appear by ten, I'll give you a knock with some tea – you'll be acclimatised by tomorrow afternoon!'

So glad I'd left my PJs in the side pocket of my travel bag. Within half an hour, I was asleep.

Having got to sleep so quickly, my messed-up body clock had me awake at 2.00am, but being so tired, after a wakeful hour or so, I managed to get another five hours.

Forcing myself out of bed before my brain had chance to talk me out of it, I stumbled towards the shower and was nearly dressed by the time I heard a quiet knock

'You're up, I'm impressed! Did you sleep okay? Take this: Matty and I will be in the kitchen making a start on the veg., then when you've had some breakfast, you can help peel the apples ready for the pie.

If you want some air after breakfast, we could use some help to decorate the porch but we shouldn't need to do much more. I'll put the turkey in early tomorrow'.

Two hours later, the porch is looking very festive, draped with greenery and festooned with pumpkins, streamers and fairy lights. It was cold though, so once I'd helped Matty spoil the new snow on the drive with our footprints, we traipsed back in, where Marlee, walking around with her phone under her chin nodded towards the carrot cake and pot of coffee on the counter.

All I could hear was 'Hm mm…. Great! I'll go move it further in before Nat and I taste the mulled wine, ciao for now, we'll see you after 4.00."

I couldn't resist

"Scuse my nosiness …I take it that was CJ?'

Marlee grinned

'Nope, another visitor… I'm going to move the car further in so the others can get past okay'.

★ ★ ★

Just before 4.30, Marlee, Matty and I were sitting in the den watching a Christmas film when I heard a car horn

'Go see who it is Matty!' she called out. As the car swept past the Lexus and around to the left, I caught a glimpse of the rear.

'It's a Bronco!' I said, feeling as excited as the child, 'Must be CJ?" as the butterflies kicked in.

Matty wasn't impressed

'Uh, uh…wrong colour… white Bronco is Grandpa – remember?'

Actually I didn't, no-one had mentioned more than one Bronco, but CJ had talked about Dad's *old* Bronco whereas this one looked pretty new.

As the doorbell rang, Matty grabbed my hand excitedly

'Come on, we need to go let Grandpa in.'

Whatever my image was of *Grandpa*, it didn't quite fit the man now standing on the porch, mid to late sixties, dark hair generously flecked with grey, *Grandpa* stamped his boots clear of snow before scooping Matty up, pretending to throw him off the porch before gently placing him back down

'So, you're the cause of all the trouble then…tell me, *what* exactly did you put in CJ's luggage?'

I must have looked nervous moments before his frown turned

into a broad smile

'Sorry, couldn't resist! Carl O 'Sullivan, AKA *Grandpa*. I don't do *Carlton* any more than CJ'

And as I held my hand out

'Don't I get a hug – I've travelled a thousand miles to meet you, left Atlanta a few hours ago. Luckily my car was already at Manchester. When I knew you were expected, I asked Marlee to put up with me for a long weekend!'

I poured more coffee and found a piece of the cake while O'Sullivan Senior greeted his ex-wife before they settled down to talk shop for a few minutes.

It must have been an hour later that, just as I'd completely forgotten, another car swept up the lane and swung into the drive, carefully edging past the Lexus and the Bronco, now several inches deep in snow.

'Daddy!' Before I knew it, Matty was off the sofa and rushing for the door again. But the man on the porch, though he looked like the photo of CJ, was on crutches, plastered upto the knee, as Matty corrected himself

'Hi Uncle Mark! Does that hurt?'

'I'm fine but stick to ski-ing Dude, don't bother with snowboarding!' Mark grinned as he hugged Matty before turning to me to

'Hi Nat... sorry I delayed my brother another day.'

I helped Mark inside and across to a high back armchair, before handing him a coffee.

'Where's Daddy hiding?'

Matty was perplexed

'He was there a few seconds ago, best go shout him but take Nat!' Mark offered

So we both grabbed our boots from by the door and stepped out. Suspiciously quiet by the car, but as we headed back towards the front door, we heard someone clearing their throat. I turned to see a figure standing in the centre of the front yard, a parcel dangling theatrically from each hand

'Which one would you like, Matty?'

He held out both and predictably, the child went for the larger one.

A dog with long floppy ears, almost as big as him. As he tore off the paper and CJ and I did our best to recover the pieces, the stranger I'd been waiting so long to meet spoke again

'So… I guess this one must be for Nat'

My unwrapping was almost as messy as Matty's. Although the second parcel was half the size of the first, there seemed to be more than one item and I was struggling to get at them.

First, I drew out a ski hat, furry lined, complete with ear flaps and tassels. Almost as bright as my fluorescent yellow pants, I looked at the label to find it came from the same shop back home.'

'Took a bit of organising. Joyce saw it and said it would match your new pants, she and I are already well acquainted…'

as he ignored my jealous *hard-Paddington* stare

'but it's the other bit I was concerned about.

Delving deeper into the package, I tore the last of the paper away to reveal …

A furry elephant…more like a woolly mammoth, wearing a stripy hat and goggles…*on skis!*

Matty was intrigued

'*Cool*… What's his name and does he make a noise…?'

Before CJ could demonstrate, his son had answered his own

question, as my new gift gave a loud trumpeting noise, clearly not lost on the next-door neighbours, nor indeed, any of those across the street who happened to be busy shovelling snow, in addition to the three figures watching from the warm, grinning through the window…

Pulling off his hat and shaking out a mass of distinctly damp hair of indeterminate colour, CJ threw off his gloves and pulled me close

'Happy Thanksgiving, *Natalie Gertrude Margarita O'Sullivan.*'

'Matty can help you think of a name, but I'm thinking *Hannibal…*

THE END

MOONTIDE

EXTRACT

Wake me at Wine Time

1

What do I remember of the accident?

Not much, aside from the deafening blare of a two-tone horn and a screech of brakes (theirs, mine or both?). Scary enough in itself, but then, boosted by the sort of grinding noise you'd get throwing a handful of nuts and bolts into a food mixer. Oh dear...

★ ★ ★

Half an hour earlier, there was me, high on life as I pulled into the next Motorway Services, just South of Birmingham. Keen to give the parents a heads-up I was on my way, I eventually located my mobile at the bottom of my thousand-complexes bag. Stepping outside, I took a deep, delicious breath of cool evening air, my first as a *Singleton* again... already loving the status if not the word.

Through to Mum, there was I, apologising that – having only left last week, they should expect me *'Around midnight – don't lock me out'*. I sensed her relief that it was over with Jean-Michel. You'd expect her to have been just a little upset... after three years.

Mais non, mes amis. (Note: But No, my friends.) Worse was to come as I heard her calling out to Dad

'George!... Lou's on her way back... they've split!'

Her attempt to muffle the phone failed to mask Dad's loud cheer. I could hear him dancing her around the kitchen; things flying off the counter; her scolding him while trying not to laugh.

WAKE ME AT WINE TIME

I'd not long cut the call, unlocking the Mini, adjusting the mirrors, changing the channel and generally getting comfortable for the long drive still ahead. With the rush hour safely behind, I was looking forward to having the motorway to myself once clear of Birmingham. But just as I was about to reverse, the phone rang again. Cursing, I cut the engine and barked into it

'Now what …?'

But this time it's not Mum. After a few seconds of silence, I can make out a male voice…indistinct, a bit shaky… and a French accent…

'Louisa, come back…

'Oh, it's you Jean-Michel… I'm a bit busy right now, can I call you later? *Doucement!* (Note: Slow down). *I'm sorry…* but I had my reasons, didn't I? No, I'm not turning round…

Then, as my voice shoots up two octaves

'No, J-M, don't do that… you have *everything* to live for! Slow down… She did what? Well, what d'you expect when you kept us both dangling! No, you mustn't… Don't please… What if it doesn't work – Imagine… you just hurt yourself but really badly. Then again, what if the fall *does* kill you? STOP IT NOW! Think of those poor Paramedics… and the Police… whoever's sent to scrape up your mess'…

I seemed to be getting through… he was already sounding calmer

'No… course I still care… how about we go for coffee when I'm back? Shall I text Fred and ask him to call you? Okay then… I'll be in touch in a couple of weeks… *Hush, now… you too… bye bye… bye… bye.'*

And with that I stuffed the phone into my bag… before cursing and retrieving it to switch it off properly. So, Jean-Michel's previous ex. (with whom he'd been two-timing me) had diverted to her personal trainer! They were welcome to each

EXTRACT

other those two, well-suited; a week ago, I'd have laughed.

Meanwhile, what did I think I was playing at? You idiot, Louisa Maxwell... at this rate you'll end up drifting back. My Instinct, regarding me over her glasses with a fierce expression, put down the Gin Martini with which she'd been celebrating my escape from London, but couldn't resist another sip, before grabbing her coat and walking out...

Trouble is, perked up with the can of caffeinated fizz I'd been swigging on my way up, turbo-charged with the strong coffee I'd had during my stop-off to keep me sharp, I'd not long re-entered the motorway when I misjudged a lane change. Pulling from the fast lane into the centre, I oversteered: just a tad was all it took as a tank-like four-wheel-drive came from nowhere. Battle-ship grey, it dwarfed the Mini, eclipsing everything in my mirrors moments before it all went dark.

2

Tumbling… it's making me feel sick… and bits of me hurt… I need to get off! I don't know how long the rolling continues before I'm aware of coming to a stop. Next there are sirens, slamming of doors, distant voices growing louder, the sounds of a door being prised open, or wrenched off… then a woman's voice, reassuring: the gentlest touch on my arm as she asks my name

'Lou… Louisa… Maxwell?…' Is this a test? I'm struggling to answer, hoping I passed.

'Okay Lou, I'm Debbie and my colleague here is Rob… you're going to be okay, my Love… I'm just going to cut your sleeve. There we go… one tiny scratch and you can go back to sleep'. *I feel the cool breeze on my arm before she gives me a shot of something… then a welcome surrender to oblivion.*

Next thing I'm aware of is waking up in hospital… reluctant to come back.

Only because I can see back is going to mean pain… and trouble… and more pain. Please let me sleep, I'm not ready… Aaaaah, that's better…

I go from the silent dark womb of cosy nothingness to an awareness of voices again… a woman… she's gently lifting my arm. Cool fingers seek my pulse as a damp cloth bathes my forehead – and face. Not Debbie this time… different accent, with an almost musical lilt… I can just make out shapes in the dimness…

'Louisa… can you hear me *Sweetheart*… Welcome back!'… Seconds later, I can hear her talking excitedly into a phone

'Jonno? *It's Patience*… Sorry to wake you but I did promise… your RTA on the Unit, she's back!'

EXTRACT

Turned out the comforting voice belonged to the Ward Sister. Her voice already soothing me, Patience herself was to be a great support in many ways during my stay: That accent of hers originally from Barbados, since spiced with a touch of Derby.

I needed reassurance as I glanced down, slurring

'What's wrong with my leg?'

Acknowledgments

Gina Fiserova – correcting my various typographical mishaps in Pigs plus tweaks to my Flash Fictions last year. This expanded collection is unapologetically cosy, aside from Iphigenia and Isabella.

Graham Hamer – author of more than 20 fast-paced, upto the moment (and at times, scarily prescient) thrillers – I love the French Collection. Your inspiring presentation 2 years ago fired me up on cracking on with my novel and getting a story or two out there. I'm proud and privileged to call you a friend (and still none the wiser on how you consistently craft such current and readable texts).

Ian Pilbeam – for the cover photograph and typography. Left to a luddite like me, this little assemblage might have remained a work-in-progress for another ten years. Thank you for sorting out the technical stuff.

Finally, my husband David. You're wonderful, holding everything together whilst your stubborn wife writes. Thanks for your indulgence during this detour from knocking the novel into shape... I promise I'll return to it soonest, and you may even get to read it before 2022 is out.

The author has asserted her right to be identified as the author of this Work in accordance with the Copyright, Designs and Patents Act 1988. No part of this book may be reproduced or transmitted in any form or by any means, graphic, electronic, or mechanical, including photocopying, recording, taping or by any information storage or retrieval system, without prior permission in writing from the author.

All characters and events featured in the stories included in this publication are fictitious and any resemblance to real persons, living or dead, is purely coincidental. Except in the case of commonly accepted historical or geographical facts, any resemblance to events, localities, actual persons – living or dead – or history of any person is entirely coincidental.

Printed in Great Britain
by Amazon